LOVE AND KISSES

As Arilla entered the room, she realized with a little constriction of her heart that there was no one there except for Lord Rochfield.

He took her hand in his and raised it to his lips and at his touch she felt herself shiver as if she were faced by a vicious serpent.

"May I say, lovely lady, that I have been looking forward to this evening."

His eyes, as he spoke, were flickering over her.

He made her feel as if her gown was transparent.

"I . . . think," said Arilla, "as your party did not . . . materialise . . . it would be correct for me to . . . leave."

Lord Rochfield laughed.

"That is something I cannot allow."

He caught her by the wrist.

"You are mine, my beautiful, and there is no escape!"

It was then that Arilla realized that she was caught in a trap.

Knowing she was lost, she could only scream and scream again . . .

A Camfield Novel of Love
by Barbara Cartland

"Barbara Cartland's novels are all distinguished by their intelligence, good sense, and good nature . . ."
> **— ROMANTIC TIMES**

"Who could give better advice on how to keep your romance going strong than the world's most famous romance novelist, Barbara Cartland?"
> **— THE STAR**

Dearest Reader,

Camfield Novels of Love mark a very exciting era of my books with Jove. They have already published nearly two hundred of my titles since they became my first publisher in America, and now all my original paperback romances in the future will be published exclusively by them.

As you already know, Camfield Place in Hertfordshire is my home, which originally existed in 1275, but was rebuilt in 1867 by the grandfather of Beatrix Potter.

It was here in this lovely house, with the best view in the county, that she wrote *The Tale of Peter Rabbit*. Mr. McGregor's garden is exactly as she described it. The door in the wall that the fat little rabbit could not squeeze underneath and the goldfish pool where the white cat sat twitching its tail are still there.

I had Camfield Place blessed when I came here in 1950 and was so happy with my husband until he died, and now with my children and grandchildren, that I know the atmosphere is filled with love and we have all been very lucky.

It is easy to write of love and I know you will enjoy the Camfield Novels of Love. Their plots are definitely exciting and the covers very romantic. They come to you, like all my books, with love.

Bless you,

Barbara Cartland

CAMFIELD NOVELS OF LOVE
by Barbara Cartland

Other books by Barbara Cartland

A NEW CAMFIELD NOVEL OF LOVE BY

BARBARA CARTLAND

Love and Kisses

JOVE BOOKS, NEW YORK

LOVE AND KISSES

A Jove Book / published by arrangement with
the author

PRINTING HISTORY
Jove edition / December 1987

ISBN: 0-515-09322-X

Jove Books are published by The Berkley Publishing Group,
200 Madison Avenue, New York, New York 10016.
The name "JOVE" and the "J" logo
are trademarks belonging to Jove Publications, Inc.

PRINTED IN THE UNITED STATES OF AMERICA

10 9 8 7 6 5 4 3 2 1

Author's Note

Duels, although frowned upon, were actually forbidden by the Victorians in the nineteenth century. They were, however, still favoured as the honourable way a gentleman settled a quarrel.

In 1809 Lord Castlereagh fought a duel with George Cannin over Government Policy and the famous Duke of Wellington fought a duel with the Earl of Winchilsea.

In 1798 William Pitt the Younger fought a duel with the Whig politician George Tierney. As Pitt was extremely thin and Tierney extremely fat, it was suggested that Pitt's outline should be chalked on Tierney's front and that any perforations outside that area should not count!

I have in my house a portrait of the beautiful but infamous Countess of Shrewsbury. She is buried in the Church of St. Giles. She was the mistress of the Second Duke of Buckingham, who was a crack shot, and between them they planned the murder of her husband.

The Countess attended the fatal duel dressed as a page-boy, and watched the Earl die from her lover's bullet. Later, she slept with the Duke, wearing her dead husband's blood-stained shirt.

chapter one

1817

Arilla looked along the unkempt drive and sighed.

She had never really expected he would come.

Yet she had hoped that he might do so.

Then as she turned despairingly back towards the house, she saw in the distance a movement.

A second later she realised it was horses.

She gave a cry of excitement.

So that she could see better, she ran up the moss-covered steps.

Some of them were broken in places, but they led to the front door.

As she turned her head again, she saw she had been right.

It was a Phaeton coming towards her drawn by a pair of perfectly matched chestnuts.

She waited and her eyes seemed to fill her small face.

They came nearer and nearer, finally drawing up with a flourish just below her.

For a moment she seemed almost speechless.

Until, as the driver of the Phaeton swept off his tall hat from his dark head, she exclaimed:

"Harry! I knew you would come!"

The gentleman gave the reins to his groom, who had climbed down from the small seat at the back of the Phaeton and jumped to the ground.

The Phaeton was a tall one.

Yet not quite so over-powering as the style the Prince Regent had introduced some years earlier.

It was lighter, better sprung, and obviously faster on the roads which, except at this time of the year, were often a quagmire after the rain.

Not hurrying himself, the gentleman walked round the Phaeton.

Then, before climbing the steps to where Arilla was waiting, he looked up at the house.

He had what she thought was a disdainful expression on his handsome face.

It was not surprising, for the stones needed pointing, and a number of the panes of glass were cracked.

The untended creepers were growing wild over many of the windows.

The gentleman, exceedingly smart with his cravat tied in an intricate pattern which Arilla guessed was the latest vogue amongst the beaux of St. James's, climbed the steps.

He said as he did so:

"Two hours exactly to reach you, and I think I have beaten my own record, unless anyone has exceeded it since I was last here?"

"No-one could drive as well as you, Harry!" Arilla replied. "And of course we have had no visitors with horses to compare with yours."

2

She saw the twist to his lips and added:

"They *are* yours?"

It was a question, and the answer was only what she had expected.

"For the day! I borrowed them, as usual!"

"Oh, Harry! Are you 'below hatches'?"

"Of course! What else did you expect?"

They walked into the hall, which was even more shabby than he remembered.

They crossed the hall into the Drawing-Room, which had once been beautiful but was now, like the rest of the house, sadly dilapidated.

The curtains were faded, the linings torn, the carpet was threadbare, and there were tell-tale marks on the walls where obviously pictures or mirrors had once hung.

Harry Vernon had put his hat and driving-gloves down in the hall as he passed through it and was now smoothing his hair with his hand.

He said in a different tone from the way he had spoken before:

"I am sorry, Arilla, to hear that your father is dead."

Arilla gave a little sigh. Then she answered, not looking at him:

"We had always been close to each other, Harry, ever since I was small, but you know it was the best thing that could have happened."

"Have things been very bad?" Harry asked sympathetically.

"It has been terrible this last year," Arilla replied.

She paused and then went on:

"Papa was in a coma and did not even recognise me. There was no money for the Doctors or for the things they wanted him to have."

Harry frowned before he said sharply:

"Why did you not let me know?"

"What would have been the use?" Arilla asked. "Unless you had come into a fortune, which was unlikely."

"Most unlikely!" he agreed. "But I would have tried to help."

"I know that," Arilla said, "but there was really nothing you could do."

She hesitated and then continued:

"I can only say, now that it is all over, and you will understand, that Papa really died a year ago."

Harry Vernon knew exactly what his cousin was saying.

When her father, Sir Roderick Lindsey, had a bad fall out hunting and was partially paralysed, he became from that moment to all intents and purposes a dead man, except that his heart was beating.

The Doctors could not rouse him into consciousness, but he went on living.

It was a tragedy for his daughter, his only child, who nursed him devotedly.

But as Harry was now aware, it was a ghastly life for her, and yet there was nothing he could do about it.

As if she could read his thoughts, Arilla said:

"Do not think about it! It is over, and now I want your help. Please, Harry, help me, because there is no-one else I can ask."

"You know I will do anything in my power," Harry answered, "which is, however, very limited."

As he spoke he walked across to the window as if he were embarrassed and looked out onto the untidy, overgrown garden.

Because it was spring the daffodils were growing in a golden carpet under the trees and the lilac and syringa were in bloom.

The garden looked beautiful, if very wild, but Harry was thinking how much he had enjoyed playing in it as a child.

He had been brought over by his father and mother to the

Manor at Little Marchwood, where he had always been welcomed by Sir Roderick and Lady Lindsey.

Sometimes, even though his father and Lady Lindsey were cousins, he had thought that she and her husband thought of him as the son they had never had.

It was, in fact, Sir Roderick who had persuaded his father, who was at times rather obstinate, that he should go to Eton.

It was Sir Roderick who had arranged for him to be accepted in the Life Guards when his father had said that he could only afford a Foot Regiment.

"I suppose," Harry thought, "it was Sir Roderick who gave me my expensive tastes."

Aloud he said:

"I will help you, of course I will help you, Arilla, but, God knows, it will not be easy."

"I am not asking you for money, Harry."

He turned round so that she could see the surprise in his eyes.

"But, surely . . .?" he began.

"Will you let me tell you what I have planned to do and why I need your help?"

"Yes, of course," Harry agreed.

"But first you must have a drink," Arilla said. "I should have suggested it before, but I was so excited to see you."

She smiled up at him as she continued:

"There is just one bottle of Papa's best claret left which I hid away—otherwise the Doctors would have drunk it—and kept for the next time you should visit us."

"Do not make me feel more guilty than I feel already!" Harry pleaded.

At the same time, he walked to where he knew the grog-tray stood at the far corner of the Drawing-Room.

There he saw, as he expected, a decanter of claret and a well-polished crystal glass waiting for him.

He poured it out and asked politely:

"You are not drinking with me?"

"It is all for you," Arilla said firmly, "and you are going to need it!"

"What mischief are you up to now?" Harry asked. "While I think of it, Arilla, you have grown very pretty since I last saw you."

She smiled at the compliment. It revealed the dimples in her cheeks, and her eyes, which were a very deep hyacinth blue, seemed to sparkle.

"That is something I hoped you would say."

"It is quite true!" Harry averred, sipping his claret.

He paused and then continued:

"Although you are a bit on the thin side, it is an improvement on the plump little girl I remember when I was here last!"

"Not so very little now!" Arilla flashed. "I am nineteen. Do you realise that, Harry? Nineteen! It makes me feel very old!"

"And I am twenty-seven," he said, "and getting on for being a Methuselah!"

They both laughed and Harry lowered himself carefully, because his champagne-coloured breeches were fashionably very tight, into an arm-chair.

He then put down his glass of claret.

Before she spoke Arilla picked up the decanter and placed it beside the glass on the small table.

Then, instead of sitting on the chair opposite him, she knelt on the hearth-rug beside Harry's chair and sat back on her heels.

"I want you to look at me, Harry, quite dispassionately," she said, "as if I were a stranger, and not your cousin whom you have known ever since I was in the cradle."

She turned her face towards him as she spoke and, as if he understood what she was asking, he said:

"I am speaking truthfully, Arilla, when I tell you that you are very pretty—in fact lovely!"

"Do you really think that? Really and truly?"

"If you bought a new gown and had your hair done in a fashionable manner, you would be sensational!"

He saw the light in her eyes and thought perhaps he was being a fool.

What was the point of telling her what was the truth when the only people to admire her, apart from the birds and the bees, were a few old clodhoppers!

There was nothing else in Little Marchwood, which he had always thought was the "back of beyond."

"That is what I hoped you would say," Arilla murmured in a rapt little voice as if she spoke to herself, "and, because I am said to be like Mama, I thought I could not be mistaken."

"You are not mistaken!" Harry said. "But what can you do about it in this 'dead-and-alive' hole? Is there anybody new in the neighbourhood?"

"What are you asking," Arilla said, "is if there are any men here whom I might marry, and the answer, quite frankly, is 'No'!"

Harry frowned and she knew he was wondering if it would be possible for him to bring any men down from London to meet her.

Knowing that even if he did so, it would be unlikely that Arilla could provide them with a decent meal and not even a drink if this was her father's last bottle of claret.

"Surely," he asked aloud, "now that your father is dead, you have a relation with whom you could live?"

Arilla laughed.

"You know all my relations as well as I do! They are either so old that they have one foot in the grave or else they are as poor as we are."

She paused and then added:

7

"Things have not changed, Harry, since we were children, and your relations, with the exception of the Duke, are in the same plight."

"The Duke!"

Harry spoke with a note of scorn in his voice, then he said:

"I have a story about His Grace's latest meanness, and about the way the Marquess economises on tips, but I will tell you that later. Let us go on talking about you."

Arilla made a note in her mind not to forget to ask Harry about his cousin, who was head of the Vernon family and had always been a source of some amusement to them all.

The Duke of Vernonwick was considered to be the meanest man in England. He had never been known to help pay any of his family in whatever straits they might find themselves.

It was a family joke amongst the Vernons to collect stories about him, only some of which were exaggerated, and pass them around.

Harry remembered his father had once said bitterly:

"The only thing the Duke has ever given us is a laugh at his expense!"

No one knew better than Arilla that Harry's father and mother, before they died, had been as poor as her own.

Harry was part of the rich, extravagant *Beau Monde* simply because, although he was impoverished, he did belong to an old family.

Added to this, he was so attractive and good-looking that the Prince Regent had constituted him one of his intimate friends.

"To get back to where we started!" Arilla said. "You tell me I am pretty and that, if I were properly dressed, I would look as lovely as Mama."

She paused and then went on:

"Well, that is why I have decided to come to London!"

Harry stared at her. Then he asked:

"How can you possibly do that?"

"That is what I am going to tell you," Arilla replied, "and why I need your help."

She settled herself a little more comfortably on the hearth-rug and said:

"I have decided that, unless I am to stay here and starve, the only thing I can do is to marry a rich man!"

Harry opened his mouth to speak and closed it again as Arilla went on:

"As you have already pointed out, I am not likely to find one falling out of the sky in Little Marchwood."

She smiled and then continued:

"There is not a chance of there being a carriage-accident outside our gates so that I can nurse its wealthy occupant back to health. Those things happen only in novelettes."

Harry thought this was true, but he did not interrupt, and Arilla went on:

"So what I intend to do is to come to London and, with your help, become an 'Incomparable.'"

"But—that is impossible!" Harry expostulated. "You do not understand. . . ."

"Wait a minute," Arilla said, putting up her hand. "I have not finished. Of course I know I cannot be an 'Incomparable' looking as I do now."

She paused and then went on:

"I know, too, that if I came to London and tried to have a Season as a *débutante,* I would have to find a chaperone and incur a great many expenses which I could not possibly afford."

"Then how . . .?" Harry began once again, only to be silenced once more as Arilla continued:

"I have therefore decided that I shall come to London, not as myself, but as the young widow of the late Sir Roderick Lindsey."

9

Now Harry was so astounded that he had no words with which to interrupt. He only stared at his cousin as if she had taken leave of her senses.

"That is exactly what I said and what I mean!" Arilla replied. "No one knows that Papa is dead except you and the people in the village."

She paused and then went on:

"As you can imagine, I did not have the money to put a notice of his deaith in the *Gazette* or the *Morning Post*.

She finished by saying:

"Quite frankly, I thought it a waste of time to notify the few relations we have who all live miles away and have never shown any particular affection for Papa."

"I can understand that," Harry said, "but unless I am very obtuse, I cannot see why you should pretend to be your father's widow."

"You are being rather foolish," Arilla replied. "As I have just said, it is far more complicated to be a *débutante* than to be a beautiful, rich widow."

"Rich?"

Harry almost shouted the question.

"That is what we will tell the world—the world in which you shine!"

Harry sat bolt upright in his chair and put his hand up to his forehead.

"I think you have gone mad! Where is this money coming from?"

"Out of my imagination—and yours."

"And what are you going to spend?"

"That is what I am going to tell you."

"And you think anyone will believe us?"

"They will believe *you*," Arilla said.

She paused and then went on:

"If you tell the people who matter and who are all friends of yours that a very attractive, quiet, well-behaved young

10

widow, who you think is very lovely, has come to London knows nobody."

She saw the disbelief in Harry's face and continued:

"You have to make them very curious about 'Lady Lindsey' and get her invited to just one or two parties, where she will be a sensation."

"Looking as you do now?" Harry asked, and his voice was hard.

"I am not as stupid as you think," Arilla replied, "and I have been planning this for a long time. In fact, ever since I realised that Papa would never get well again."

She hesitated and then continued:

"I knew that when he died I should be alone here with nobody to talk to except the poor old Johnsons who should have been retired years ago."

"The whole idea is crazy," Harry said, "but go on."

"The one thing I have never sold, and you know practically everything else worth even a few pence has gone, is Mama's pearl necklace. She left it to me and the diamond star she used to wear in the front of her gown."

There was a little sob in Arilla's voice as she went on:

"Because I loved them and because they were now mine, I clung on to them, never contemplating selling them, until I realised that they could constitute my *entrée* into another world."

Arilla paused and then went on:

"It is the world Mama had always wanted me to enjoy if only we had the money. I really think it was she who put this idea into my head."

Harry did not speak and, after a moment, Arilla said:

"In fact, I am sure of it! I often feel Mama is near me, and I know this is what she would want me to do."

"I cannot believe that your mother would expect you to attempt the impossible."

"Why is it so impossible?" Arilla asked aggressively.

11

"Think of it, Harry: you said I am pretty and I shall have enough money, if I am careful, to buy clothes in which you will not be ashamed of me."

She finished by saying:

"I can make my money last for a little over two months."

"I thought you said you were supposed to be rich?" Harry asked.

Arilla laughed, and it was a very pretty sound.

"I thought you would question that, but you know as well as I do that rich people never throw their money about."

She paused and then said:

"Just think how many people you have been told are rich who have given you hardly any sign of it."

"I suppose that is true."

"There are other people as peculiar as the Duke. Think of Lord Barlow, who lived near here and who was reputed to be enormously wealthy."

Arilla looked up at Harry as she continued:

"He never gave sixpence to any charity and, when he entertained, Papa said his food was inedible and the wine so cheap as to be an insult!"

There was a pause, then Harry said after a moment:

"You have certainly got something there. Now I come to think of it, there are quite a number of people in London whom I know to be rich but certainly do not appear to spend their money at all freely."

"The only rich person I ever knew was my Godmother," Arilla said, "who would send me a card at Christmas which she had received the year before from somebody else!"

Harry laughed, and Arilla went on:

"You do see, therefore, Harry, that all you have to do is to get it into people's minds that the beautiful 'Lady Lindsey' is rich."

She paused and then continued:

"They will not expect any concrete evidence of it, except that she is well-dressed."

"And where do you intend to stay in London?" Harry asked.

Arilla looked at him quickly, then away again before she said:

"I thought . . . perhaps . . . you could help me there. If I rent a house for two months . . . I would not have much money left to spend on . . . clothes for myself!"

"Well, there you are then!" Harry said as if he were pleased to find a snag in what was obviously a high-flown fairy story.

Then, as he saw the disappointment in Arilla's eyes, he said:

"Wait a minute! I have an idea!"

"You have?" Arilla asked excitedly.

"When I received your letter saying that your father was dead and that you wished to see me, I had just been saying good-bye to a friend who was leaving for Paris for two months."

Arilla did not interrupt, but there was an expression of hope in her eyes that was very touching.

"My friend is not of the *Beau Monde* and not somebody I could introduce to you! But she has been well set up in a very elegant house in Islington."

Harry went on:

"She told me that if I were pressed for accommodation while she was away, I could stay there and it would give the servants something to do."

"Oh, Harry! And you think . . ." Arilla started to say.

"It is certainly a possibility," Harry interrupted, "for the only expense would be the food you eat and of course the generous tip you would be expected to give the servants for looking after you."

Arilla gave a little cry of delight. Then, moving on her knees towards Harry, she said:

"Are you saying . . . are you really telling me that you . . . will do this . . . for me?"

"I think it is a mad, crazy, ridiculous idea!" Harry replied. "But I suppose it is better than sitting here and turning into a cabbage!"

"Oh, Harry . . . !"

The tears were in Arilla's large eyes. Then, as if she could not prevent them, they overflowed and ran down her cheeks.

She put her arms on his knees and looked up at him to say in a broken little voice:

"I . . . I always knew you were the . . . kindest . . . most . . . wonderful . . . cousin that . . . anybody could have!"

"Do not thank me yet!" Harry said quickly. "We may have decided to run in the race, but there are a hell of a lot of obstacles in front of us before we reach the winning-post!"

Arilla wiped away her tears with the back of her hand in a childlike gesture before she said:

"I know that, but anything I gain we share."

"What do you mean?" Harry asked, and she thought there was an ominous note in his voice.

"Now, do not be proud and stupid," she said. "We shared things when we were children and we will share them again now. I am not going to have any arguments about it!"

"Well, I am!" Harry declared. "So you had better explain a little more fully what you mean!"

"I mean that if I marry a rich man, I shall see to it that you have a great many things you cannot afford now."

Harry would have spoken but she put up her fingers and pressed them against his lips.

"We are in this together, Harry, win or lose, and if you refuse to do it my way, then I shall just sit here and cry alone among the cabbages until—as you have already suggested—I turn into one!"

Harry laughed as if he could not help himself. Then he said:

"It is no use quarreling over what may never happen and, if after two months you are left on my hands, I shall have to dispose of you to the 'Rag-and-Bone Man'!"

"It is not going to be as bad as that," Arilla said, "and it will make it easier for me if I am not working just for myself."

She paused and then continued:

"I hate to think of you having to sponge on a lot of people simply because you cannot afford to dress as you do, or ride horses which are your own, or keep yourself as the gentleman you are!"

"If you talk like that," Harry joked, "I shall burst into tears! Stop it, Arilla!"

He laughed and then said:

"Let us sit down and work out this fairy story so that we make no mistakes and are not seized by an Ogre or eaten by some fiery Dragon the moment you set foot in London!"

"If you will help me . . . I will . . . not be so . . . afraid," Arilla said.

"I will help you because you have asked me to do so," he answered, "although, God knows, I think, if the truth were known, I am fit only for Bedlam!"

They both laughed, then Arilla filled up Harry's glass from the decanter and said:

"We must drink a toast to our success, and as there is only one glass, I will have to share yours, which is symbolic, if you think about it!"

"Symbolic, nothing!" Harry retorted. "It is cheese-paring, if you ask me!"

Then they were laughing again until Harry, lifting his glass of claret, said:

"To the incomparable Lady Lindsey! May she achieve everything she desires!"

He drank a little of the claret and then Arilla, taking the glass from him and holding it up as he had done, said:

"To Harry, the Archangel who will open the gates of Paradise for me!"

She drank only a little of the claret before she put the glass back on the table. Then she said, her eyes dancing with excitement:

"Now you realise you have to tell me exactly what I have to do to make sure that there is no possibility of making a mistake!"

"I will make sure of that," Harry replied, "by seeing to it that you obey me!"

"Which I have done ever since I was a little girl, when you used to make me 'fag' for you until I was so tired I could have cried!"

Arilla smiled at him and went on:

"And, if you remember, I also had to bowl for you when you were practising cricket, and it was always I who had to run to pick up the ball!"

Harry laughed.

"I used to wonder then what else girls were for!"

"And what are girls for now?" Arilla asked.

He smiled.

"That is something you will learn in London!"

*　*　*

Driving, two weeks later, in a carriage that Harry had sent for her, Arilla felt as if there were a hundred butterflies fluttering in her breast.

Although it was a warm day, her fingers felt cold.

It had been one thing to live her fantasies during the long and dismal days when her father lay upstairs unconscious and there was nobody to talk to except the old servants.

They only grumbled about their rheumatism and the extra work that the Doctors made for them every time they called.

If it had not been for her dreams, she felt she would have been very much more unhappy than she had in fact been, for they had prevented her from feeling so lonely.

She would sometimes go a whole week without speaking to anybody outside the house.

Now amazingly, and certainly excitingly, what had just been in her mind was becoming a reality.

It was with difficulty that she prevented herself from pinching her arms to make certain she was awake.

Harry had gone back to London with the jewels.

He had written to her to say that he had actually obtained for them, after a great deal of haggling, a little more than they had anticipated.

He was, therefore, sending her a gown and a bonnet in which to travel to his friend's house in Islington.

Arilla had been interested in his friend, but he had been very mysterious about her.

She had asked Harry several questions, only a few of which he had answered.

She gathered that the lady, of whom he was apparently very fond, was staying in Paris with the gentleman who had given her the house.

It seemed strange to Arilla that, without being married, a man would spend so much on somebody who Harry admitted would not be accepted, as she herself would be, by his smart friends.

Very vaguely, because living in the country she had never come in contact with such people, she knew there were women such as actresses who were taken out to supper by gentlemen like Harry.

But they were not part of the "Social Scene" in which as Lady Lindsey she wished to shine.

She felt fairly sure she would not make many social mistakes.

This was for the simple reason that her mother, who had died just before her sixteenth birthday, had been very insistent that even though they were poor, they behaved in what she called "the proper manner."

Although their meals were plain and simple, her father and mother always changed for dinner into evening-clothes.

As soon as Arilla was old enough to dine with them, she did the same.

If there was a complicated dish, her mother would slip into the kitchen to finish it off before old Johnson brought it into the Dining-Room.

Her father would then behave as if nothing untoward were taking place.

Her mother would come back, looking a little flushed but very lovely, as she sat down and continued the conversation where it had left off.

Arilla had also been taught how to receive guests and how to look after them.

Although it might be only the Vicar, the Doctor, or somebody from the village, her mother was most insistent that she should behave in exactly the right manner.

She learned to greet such ordinary guests with as much consideration as she would have greeted the Lord Lieutenant's wife, or one of her father's more distinguished relations.

If she ever made a mistake, her mother would point it out to her later.

"You must always look at people when they are introduced to you, darling," she would say.

She would continue:

"Being shy is no excuse for looking down, which is rude, as is not shaking hands at exactly the right angle."

Arilla had learned how to curtsy to the Queen, in case the

miracle her mother prayed for happened and she was presented at Court.

If not to the Queen, then to the Prince Regent, which actually Arilla thought would be far more exciting.

"Perhaps," she told herself now as the wheels carried her to London, "I shall meet the Prince Regent, as Harry is a friend of his."

Then she remembered hearing that the Prince Regent preferred older women.

A rumour had even reached the village that, before he had married Princess Caroline of Brunswick, which had been a disaster, he had been secretly married.

Although it seemed hard to believe, he was purported to have been married to a Mrs. Fitzherbert, who was older than His Royal Highness.

"Whomever he has married, it would still be exciting to meet him!" Arilla thought.

Then she remembered she had to concentrate on finding a rich husband.

'If I do so, I shall make quite certain that somehow I shall be able to pay off Harry's debts and at least give him a horse of his own and pay a groom to look after it.'

She had known every time Harry came to visit them how much he disliked having to rely on his friends for a vehicle to carry him from London down to Little Marchwood.

She knew he was a magnificent rider. She had been very proud, too, that, after the Battle of Waterloo, he had been awarded by the Duke of Wellington a medal for gallantry.

"It is a tragedy that Harry has to leave the Regiment," her father had said when the war ended.

"Why does he have to do that, Papa?" she asked.

"Because he cannot afford it."

He gave a little sigh before he added:

"It is my fault. He should have gone into a Foot Regiment, which would have been cheaper."

He paused and then continued:

"But as he rode so well and was so good-looking, I wanted him to be in my own Regiment, where I knew he would make his mark."

"Yes, Harry must have horses!" Arilla told herself.

"Although his relatives have not helped him, I will make sure that my husband becomes as fond of him as I am."

She continued to think about Harry.

"He will always have a home with us, horses to ride, as well as a place where he can entertain his friends."

It was difficult to have a clear picture of the man she might marry, envisaging him as perhaps a benevolent older man.

Maybe somebody like her father who, as her mother had often said, would have given the shirt off his back if she had not prevented it.

"Your father should have been a rich man," she once said to Arilla.

She went on to explain:

"He is so kind and generous in thought, word, and deed and that, darling, is the reason why I love him."

"Then he is certainly rich, Mama!" Arilla exclaimed.

Her mother smiled.

"I know that, and we have so much more than money can buy."

She thought Arilla looked puzzled and she said:

"I am talking about love. The love I have for your father and which he has for me and which, darling, we have for you. I thank God every day for my adorable little daughter."

When her mother died, Arilla had thought the sunshine had left the house, and she knew that her father would never be the same again.

At first he had been unapproachable, then his character and behaviour seemed to change radically.

He rode recklessly, he drank too much, and would often be

sharp and unkind to her because, as she knew, she looked like the wife he had lost.

She was quite certain that when he had his accident he was riding in a reckless fashion simply because in some way that alleviated a little the pain that was in his heart.

At first, after they had brought him home on a gate, which was the easiest way to carry him, Arilla had cried despairingly.

She could not believe she would lose her father so soon after losing her mother.

"Please, God, do not let him die!" she prayed. "If he does, I shall be all alone . . . completely and absolutely . . . alone!"

Then as her father lingered on, not, she thought, as himself, but just a body from which the spirit had already flown, she knew that death would be a blessed release.

Not only for him but also for herself.

It was so upsetting to watch him lying still, just as handsome as he had always been, yet knowing he could not hear her when she spoke to him and would make no answer.

She had known when the Doctors came out of his room shaking their heads that there was nothing they could do.

As the weeks turned into months she began to feel as if she were losing not only him, but the spirit of life itself so that she, too, was becoming just a body.

Then, almost as if her mother comforted her, she began to pray that once she was free she would not let the restrictions of her present existence defeat her.

"I will live, Mama, as you wanted me to do if we could have afforded it. Even if for just a short while, a few weeks, a month, everything might change."

The story grew more elaborate as she added to it and examined every action, every step she should make in order to be a social success.

Because she knew it would please her mother, she prac-
tised in front of her mirror the movements she had taught her.

This would help her to be graceful in the way she used her
hands, in the way she walked, and in the way she spoke.

She forced herself to keep up with local affairs, to follow
what was happening in Parliament, and to understand the
general condition of the country.

It was not easy because it would have been extravagant,
when every penny counted, to buy newspapers.

But she knew that the Vicar took one newspaper, and a
retired Bank Manager who lived in the village another.

A third and somewhat "scurrilous rag," according to her
father, was read by the Butcher.

It had been embarrassing and somewhat humiliating to ask
all three men to keep their newspapers for her to read after
they had finished with them.

The Vicar had stipulated that she should collect his copy of
The Times when it was three days old.

The retired Bank Manager, who enjoyed reading *The
Morning Post*, wanted two days.

The Butcher said firmly that she could have the weekly
Reformists Register a week after he had read it and he would
try to remember not to wrap meat in it.

Sometimes he would forget.

However, because he had been fond of her father and had
always tried to please her mother, he would then be most
apologetic.

He would give her the newspaper which Arilla suspected
he had not yet finished reading himself.

She was not prepared to argue, whatever happened, because it was such a joy to read what was happening in the
outside world.

It sometimes seemed to her as if in her village they were
living on a different planet from that about which she was
reading.

But it gave her a chance to think out the intelligent questions she intended to ask, provided there was somebody there to answer them.

She also thought that the men and women with whom Harry associated would be witty and amusing and that was what she would have to be.

She hoped and prayed she would have a chance of shining amongst such people who were very different from anybody she had ever known.

"Help me, Mama, you will . . . have to help me!" she told her mother in her heart.

She hoped, too, when she thought how dashing her father must have looked when he was a young man in the Life Guards, that he would understand.

Now the miracle she had prayed and hoped for was becoming a reality, and she was travelling to London.

It was a very smart carriage that Harry had sent for her and the coachman wore a tiered cape and the footman a distinctive livery.

She imagined it as a chariot that would carry her across the sky into the heart of the sun.

"I have to look and feel like a goddess," she told herself, and thought in fact she already looked like one.

Harry had sent her a gown that was very different from the plain muslin ones she usually wore at home, which were faded and threadbare if she had not outgrown them.

The gown he had chosen was the blue of the sky, trimmed with braid in an intricate design, and had long sleeves with frills falling over her hands.

Waists were still high as they had been during the war. Arilla had heard that decoration on gowns was becoming more and more elaborate.

Her bonnet was certainly very different from anything she had ever seen in Little Marchwood.

It had blue ribbons to tie under her chin, the brim was

edged with lace, and small tightly curled ostrich feathers decorated the crown.

When she looked at herself in the mirror she could hardly believe she was not seeing a complete stranger.

But she knew, without being conceited, that she was very pretty.

'I shall not let Harry down,' she thought.

This was the beginning of a great adventure.

Whatever happened in the future, she would never regret taking part in it.

chapter two

The carriage drew up outside an attractive-looking house in Islington. Arilla was so excited that for the moment it was impossible to move.

Then when the footman, having got down from the box had rung the bell, the door opened.

There was quite a little pause before Arilla stepped elegantly out of the carriage to find a smart-looking parlour-maid with a frilled apron and cap to match waiting to let her in.

"Good morning!" she said as the parlour-maid curtsied.

"Good mornin', M'Lady! I 'opes you 'ad a good journey!"

"Very good, thank you."

She was not certain whether she should thank the coach-man and footman or whether they were waiting, so she just walked into the hall and asked:

"Is Mr. Vernon here?"

"He's waitin' for Your Ladyship in th' Drawing-Room," the parlour-maid said, going ahead of her.

It was difficult for Arilla to walk slowly rather than run as she wanted to do to find Harry.

She was suddenly frightened at what she had undertaken. She knew she would feel safe only if she could hold on to him and hear him telling her everything was all right.

The room into which she was shown was very elegant and looked out onto a small garden at the back.

Harry was standing at the window thinking, Arilla felt perceptively, not of what he was seeing but of what they were going to do now that she had arrived.

"Lady Lindsey, Sir!" the parlour-maid announced.

Harry turned and Arilla could now run across the room towards him.

"I am . . . here! I . . . am here!" she cried. "Oh, Harry . . . have we made . . . a mistake?"

Harry smiled, then, holding her by the shoulders at arm's length, he said:

"Let me look at you!"

Arilla looked up at him apprehensively, her eyes worried as he searched her face, then looked down at her gown.

"Perfect!" he said. "Exactly how I wanted you to look!"

"Oh, Harry, are you sure?"

"Very sure," he replied, "and you must have confidence in yourself, Arilla, otherwise you will not be able to 'put it over,' as one might say."

"Oh, I will! I will!" Arilla said. "But I am so afraid of letting . . . you down."

"It would be more a case of letting yourself down," he said. "What do you think of your background?"

For a moment she did not realise he meant the house. Then she looked at the large high-ceilinged room which ran the whole length of the house.

The furniture, covered in blue brocade, was in excellent taste, and an elegant crystal chandelier hung from the ceiling.

There were several impressive pictures on the walls.

Arilla thought they were reproductions of pictures she knew were in the National Gallery, or else in the Capitals of Europe.

"It is well 'up to scratch'!" she enthused, using a slang phrase which made Harry laugh.

"You may be sure of that," he said, "for Barlow's taste is excellent!"

"Barlow?" she enquired.

"The name of the gentleman who is your host, although he is unaware of it."

Arilla looked puzzled.

"I thought you said it was a lady who lived here."

There was a little pause before Harry asked indifferently:

"What does it matter? But in case people ask you questions, it is Lord Barlow's house and he has rented it to you while he is abroad, because he knew your husband."

Arilla drew in her breath.

"I do hope I shall remember all these things."

"You will," Harry said confidently, "and now, the first thing you have to do is to buy some new clothes."

He paused and then continued:

"I have already ordered a dressmaker to come here immediately we have finished luncheon."

"Here?" Arilla asked in surprise. "I thought we would go to a shop."

"That would be a mistake. I do not want anybody to see you until you burst on them like a comet on an unsuspecting world!"

"I think you are teasing me!" Arilla said in a small voice. "And when is . . . that to . . . happen?"

"Tomorrow evening," Harry said. "I have arranged to

introduce you to one of the most important hostesses in London."

He looked at her and then added:

"If you make yourself pleasant, and it is very important that you should, she may give you a ticket for Almacks."

Arilla knew that Almacks was the most important and the most exclusive Club.

It was here that all the glittering lights of the *Beau Monde*, of which Harry was one, danced and met their friends.

She knew if she was accepted at Almacks she would be accepted by every hostess in England.

In a rather shy voice she asked:

"Who . . . am I meeting tomorrow evening?"

"The Countess of Jersey," Harry replied. "She is a difficult woman and unpredictable. She can 'make or break' you and that is why she is so important."

What Harry said did nothing to build up Arilla's confidence.

Not even when they sat down in the Dining-Room to a delicious luncheon at which Harry was obviously appreciating the excellent claret.

Only when the servants were not in the room did Arilla ask in a whisper:

"How much do we have to pay for all this? I am sure it is very expensive!"

"Leave all those arrangements to me," Harry said. "You have a staff which consists of a Cook, a parlour-maid, and a house-maid—all women!"

He laughed as he went on:

"Apparently when Barlow comes here he brings his own man-servant to wait on him, so you will have to manage without a Butler!"

Again Arilla thought it rather puzzling, if it was Lord Barlow's house, that Harry should talk about his "coming here" as if it were just an occasional visit.

She thought it however a mistake to ask too many questions.

Before luncheon Arilla had gone upstairs to tidy herself up and take off her bonnet.

She had been thrilled by the luxury and the attractiveness of the bedroom in which she was to sleep.

Never had she imagined anything so alluring as the silk curtains which draped the bed and the dressing table with its flounce of real lace.

The mirrors seemed to magnify and multiply the room until it was difficult to move without seeing herself reflected at a dozen different angles.

The house-maid who helped her was an attractive young woman who was obviously very impressed by her title.

"Do I look all right?" Arilla asked her when she was ready to go downstairs.

"Yer looks lovely, M'Lady an' a real lady, if I may say so!"

Arilla thought that was a strange thing to say but she made no comment.

She was too busy thanking Harry for finding her such a lovely house to ask him for an explanation.

Only when luncheon was finished and they returned to the Drawing-Room did she say a little anxiously:

"We must be very careful not to spend too much money on my clothes. It would be sad if all this should come abruptly to an end sooner than we anticipated."

"What I have done," Harry explained, "is to promise the dressmaker that you will tell anyone who admires your gowns who designed them for you."

He paused and then added:

"I know the dressmaker has made quite a number of gowns for the person who usually lives here."

Arilla looked at him enquiringly, and he said:

"To put it bluntly, if the dressmaker lets you have clothes

cheaply, you are expected to reciprocate by sending her new and important customers."

Harry started to say:

"Most of those she has been dressing so far are Cyp—"

But at the last moment he changed it to:

". . . actresses."

"Now I understand what you are saying," Arilla said. "Because she thinks I am a 'Lady of Quality,' she hopes through me to dress the ladies of the *Beau Ton*."

"Exactly!" Harry replied.

"But . . . supposing nobody . . . admires me?"

"They will," Harry said confidently, "and we must make sure they do."

* * *

When the dressmaker arrived, Arilla was surprised to find that she was a comparatively young and very attractive woman.

"Here I am, Mr. Vernon," she said as Harry shook hands with her, "and, as usual, you've coaxed me into doing you a favour."

She laughed as she said:

"I asked myself on the way here why I'm so stupid as to listen to your honeyed tongue!"

"Now, you are being unkind to me, Liza!" Harry complained. "I promise you will lose nothing by helping me to make Lady Lindsey the success she is bound to be."

The dressmaker turned towards Arilla.

She gave her a searching look which seemed to take in her face, her hair, her figure, all in the space of a fleeting glance.

Then she smiled and said to Harry: "All right, you win!" before she curtsied.

Arilla had always thought that buying clothes, if only she had the money to do so, would be an exciting experience.

What she had not expected, however, was that it would be such a tiring one.

She had put on over a dozen different gowns which the dressmaker had brought with her.

By the time she had run up and down the stairs to her bedroom to do so, her legs were aching and she wanted to sit down and rest.

It was harder work than riding all day, Arilla decided, or even waiting on her father, which had been hard enough.

What was more, she saw Harry in a new guise, and had no idea how he could possibly be so knowledgeable about a woman's appearance.

He suggested little alterations and amendments to almost every gown, and extraordinarily enough his suggestions met with Liza's approval.

"Now, why didn't I think of that?" she asked as Harry suggested improvements to a Ball gown of pale green gauze which was like the first leaves of spring.

He insisted that it would be greatly improved if there were water-lilies, with their magnolia-like petals, round the hem and two small ones on the shoulders.

"You are right! Of course you are right!" she said when Harry refused one gown altogether.

He said it was too old for Arilla and dull, making her look like the wife of a City Alderman.

But the majority of the gowns were so becoming that Arilla found herself wondering which she should choose.

She thought it would be very difficult to decide that one suited her more than another.

When finally, after discarding two of the gowns which Liza had brought with her, Harry said they would take the rest, Arilla stared at him in utter astonishment.

"Are you . . . saying I should really . . . have all . . . these," she asked in a voice that did not sound like her own.

"We will need a few more," Harry said, "and Liza will bring you sketches and samples of those tomorrow."

"B-but . . . I cannot . . . it is quite . . . impossible!" Arilla objected frantically.

Then, as Harry frowned at her, her voice died away and she could only look on helplessly.

Harry arranged with the dressmaker to have two gowns delivered later that evening and most of the others the next day before luncheon.

Only when Liza had left and the maids were carrying her gowns out to the carriage outside did Arilla say, as Harry came back into the room:

"Are you mad? How can we possibly afford all those gowns? I am sure I shall never have the chance to wear them all!"

Harry shut the door and now he came to where she was standing on the hearth-rug, looking so frightened that she was trembling a little.

"Now, listen to me, Arilla," he said. "Either you allow me to be in charge or, if you prefer to do things your way, I will just leave you to it."

Arilla gave a cry of horror.

"No, no . . . I did not . . . mean that! You know I could not manage on . . . my own! But . . . all those gowns . . . will . . . cost a fortune!"

"Which the 'rich Lady Lindsey' can well afford!" Harry said, accentuating the adjective.

Then as if the way she stared at him made him realise how young and frightened she was, he said:

"Leave everything to me! I promise it will be all right, and you will not suddenly find yourself deeply in debt and the Duns threatening you!"

"B-but we have . . . so little money."

"Have you forgotten?" Harry asked. "It is the 'sprat to

catch a mackerel,' but the sprat has to be attractive and, more than anything else, has to look rich!"

Arilla did not speak and he put his arm in a brotherly way around her shoulders.

"Do not worry," he said. "You are going to be a huge success and once you find your Prince, the whole fairy story will come true and you will live happily ever after!"

"Perhaps it is . . . asking . . . too much!" Arilla said in a very small voice.

"Nonsense!" Harry said positively. "When you arrived I knew we were gambling on a certainty!"

"Are you . . . sure of . . . that?" Arilla whispered.

Harry looked at her and he said:

"To tell the truth, I am beginning to enjoy myself!"

He paused and then went on:

"If there is one thing which will be really satisfactory, it will be to deceive all those people who are so confident and pleased with themselves that they think they know everything."

He smiled as he said:

"If we can take them 'for a ride,' we will be the ones who are laughing!"

The way he spoke with a lilt in his voice made Arilla's spirits rise.

"You really . . . think we can . . . do this?" she asked.

"When I see you looking as you do now, I am sure of it!" Harry said. "Do you know what Liza said to me when she was leaving?"

Harry paused, as if to make what he was about to say more sensational.

"Liza said to me: 'You're on to a good thing, Mr. Vernon. She's rich and she's the loveliest person I've seen in a long time! Be careful you don't lose her.'"

Arilla drew in her breath.

"Did she really say that?"

"She did, and you can be quite certain, having bought your clothes from her, that she will boast about you to everybody she serves."

He added:

"By tomorrow evening, quite a considerable number of people will be talking about you."

"It sounds frightening," Arilla said, "but at the same time exciting!"

"It is exciting!" Harry agreed.

He paused and then continued:

"But, remember, the thing which is really important is to make sure that we are completely convincing in the parts we play so that no one can find holes in them."

Arilla thought for a moment. Then she said:

"If I am . . . supposed to be so rich . . . will not Liza . . . if that is her name . . . think it . . . strange that you 'bargained' . . . over the price of my gowns?"

"You are not to let that worry you," Harry said. "I explained to Liza that despite being rich, your husband, who is now dead, was extremely mean."

He went on to say:

"I told her that he therefore gave you only a small dress allowance and you have not yet got used to spending the very large fortune he left you."

Harry smiled as he continued:

"I was quite eloquent on how it would be a great mistake for her to frighten you by London prices, which are very different from anything you have paid in the country."

Arilla thought for a moment. Then she said:

"The gown I wore when I arrived looked very expensive, and you have not yet told me how much you paid for the bonnet that went with it."

"You need not worry about them," Harry said. "They cost nothing!"

"Nothing? What do you mean?" Arilla enquired.

"I borrowed them from one of my less respectable friends," Harry said, "and when you have your own things, Arilla, I will take them back."

"Oh, Harry, how could you? And how can I tell the lady to whom they belonged how grateful I am?"

"I will do that for you," Harry promised. "Incidentally, like my friend who lives in this house, she is someone else to whom I would not introduce you."

"And yet . . . they are . . . friends of yours?"

"That is different, as you well know."

"I suppose what you are saying is that they are actresses," Arilla said, thinking that would explain why the lady in question had such very pretty clothes.

There was a little pause before Harry said:

"That is right."

Because she knew him so well, Arilla had a suspicion that he was lying, but she could not think why.

When Harry left her to go back to his lodgings and change, he told her he would come back to dine with her.

"I should like that, if it is not very boring for you to be alone with me," Arilla said humbly. "But, if you are busy, I shall be all right alone."

"I will sacrifice myself!" he answered lightly. "As a matter of fact, I have quite a lot of things to tell you about the people you will meet tomorrow."

He paused and then went on:

"It is a good thing to be prepared. I do not want you to make any mistakes which might prove embarrassing."

"No, no! Of course not!" Arilla said quickly.

When Harry had left, she went upstairs feeling rather tired.

The house-maid, whose name was Rose, suggested that she should get into bed and have a rest before she brought in her bath.

Such luxury sounded so inviting that Arilla did what she

35

said, and almost as soon as her head touched the pillow she fell asleep.

That was not surprising, considering she had been awake most of the previous night, worrying not only about what lay ahead, but also over what she was leaving behind.

She had given the Johnsons their small wages and all the ready money she had left, so that they could buy food.

She was determined to ask Harry if she could send them a little extra every week.

Arilla knew only too well that for a long time there had not really been enough food in the house to feed three people as well as providing what was ordered by the Doctors for her father.

"As soon as I marry my rich husband," she told herself, "I will pension the Johnsons off generously."

She continued to think about them:

"They can either stay at the Manor, if I keep it, or I will provide them with a cottage in the village."

She thought with a sigh that, when this rich man materialised, there were such a lot of things she wanted to do with his money.

There were people like the Grocer and the Butcher, who had been kind and given her credit when things were more difficult than usual.

She would like to reward them with a present, or, if it was possible, enough money for them to take a holiday.

In fact, when she began to count them up, there were at least a dozen people she wanted to benefit by her good fortune if it ever really came her way.

But she had the uncomfortable feeling that what she planned to spend on them would amount to quite a considerable sum.

It would be unfortunate if the dream-husband proved to be cheese-paring and mean, as were the rich people she had talked about to Harry.

"In which case, I shall not marry him!" she told herself firmly, and wondered if she would have any choice in the matter.

Rose woke her to say that her bath was ready.

It had been brought into the bedroom and set down in front of the fire which had been lit.

Cans of hot water and cold were standing beside it, and Arilla began to feel that she really was a Princess in a fairy tale.

By the time she had put on one of the evening-gowns which Harry had bought for her from Liza she was quite sure of it.

Never had she imagined she could look so glamorous, so different from the girl with untidy hair wearing old cotton dresses who had lived all her life in Little Marchwood.

The gauze gown, which revealed the slimness of her figure beneath it, she felt was immodestly low in the *décolletage*.

Yet it was so elegant that she was afraid the reflection she saw of herself in the mirror was just an illusion.

At any moment she would come back to reality.

When she went downstairs to wait for Harry she could see herself reflected in the gilt-framed mirrors in the Drawing-Room.

Arilla found it difficult not to pose in front of them, and in fact be entranced by her own appearance.

Because it was still chilly in the evenings, although during the day it had been warm, a fire had been lit in the Drawing-Room.

She was standing in front of it when the door opened and with a leap of her heart she thought that Harry had arrived.

Instead, the parlour-maid announced:

"Lord Rochfield, M'Lady!"

To Arilla's surprise a distinguished-looking man came into the room.

37

It flashed through her mind that Harry might have asked him to dine with them.

Then, as he advanced towards her, she was aware that Lord Rochfield was looking at her with the same surprise in his eyes that must have been in hers.

"Good evening!" he said as he reached her. "Are you a friend of Mimi's?"

"Mimi?" Arilla questioned.

She thought that Lord Rochfield must have been expecting to see the real owner of the house rather than herself, and she said quickly:

"I am staying here, but there is nobody else in the house."

"Has Mimi gone? That is certainly a surprise," Lord Rochfield exclaimed, "but I am sure in the circumstances you will console me for her absence."

Arilla looked puzzled. Then before she could speak he went on:

"You are lovely! I cannot think why I have not seen you before."

There was something in the way he was looking at her which made Arilla feel uncomfortable.

She was not aware that as he approached her, because she was standing in front of the fire, her body beneath her gauze gown was silhouetted against it.

Now she was vividly conscious that ther *décolletage* was very low as she had thought from the first, and the expression in Lord Rochfield's eyes was somehow impertinent.

"I am . . . sorry if you are . . . disappointed in not . . . finding the lady you . . . expected . . ." she began.

"I am not disappointed now," Lord Rochfield interrupted, "for I can see, my dear, now that I look at you, that you are much more attractive than Mimi."

He paused and then went on:

"In fact, I find you irresistibly alluring, as I shall explain a little later when we have had dinner."

He hesitated, and Arilla had the frightening idea that he was about to touch her and she took a step backwards.

"Are we dining here," Lord Rochfield asked, "or do you want me to take you to the White House?"

"I . . . I must try to explain . . ." Arilla said in a nervous little voice.

"There is no need for explanations," Lord Rochfield said. He laughed and went on:

"I shall be content to be with anyone so lovely wherever we find ourselves. And as quickly as possible in bed!"

Arilla stared at him in horror.

Then to her utter relief at that moment the door opened and she heard the parlour-maid say:

"Mr. Vernon, M'Lady!"

"Harry Vernon!" he exclaimed. "What the devil are you doing here?"

"I might ask you the same question!" Harry replied, and his voice was sharp.

"Now, look here," Lord Rochfield said, "I told Mimi I would be calling on her this evening, but I understand she has provided me with a substitute in the shape of this very pretty lady."

Harry had reached the hearth-rug by this time, and because she was frightened, Arilla put out her hand to hold on to his arm.

"What you do not understand, My Lord," he said to Lord Rochfield, "is that Mimi has gone to Paris and my cousin, Lady Lindsey, has rented the house from Barlow in her absence."

Lord Rochfield looked astonished and glanced at Arilla suspiciously, as if he thought he was being deceived.

However, seeing that she really was frightened, which convinced him that Harry was speaking the truth, he said:

"I see there has been a misunderstanding."

"It is not your fault," Harry said, "and Mimi should

certainly have told you before she left England of her change of plan."

He spoke in a somewhat lofty tone.

Then Arilla could see that a thought had come into his mind that had not been there before, and his attitude changed.

"I must explain, My Lord," he said, "that my cousin has always lived very quietly in the country. Then, very soon after her marriage, she very tragically became a widow."

Harry paused and then continued:

"This is, therefore, the first time she has been to London, and I hope you will not upset her, seeing that you are the first member of London society to whom she has been introduced."

"It is certainly a unique situation!" Lord Rochfield said.

"Let me offer you a drink," Harry said. "There should be a bottle of champagne here."

He walked across the room as he spoke, leaving Arilla behind with Lord Rochfield standing beside her.

"I hope you will forgive me if I offended you before knowing who you were," he said politely.

"Of . . . course I will," Arilla replied. "I was just . . . bewildered because I do not even . . . know the name of the . . . lady who lives in this . . . house."

Lord Rochfield gave a little cough and said in a different tone:

"As you are new to London, although I am sure your cousin will introduce you to many interesting people, I hope I may have the pleasure of taking you driving in the Park."

He smiled and then added:

"Perhaps you will both dine with me one evening."

"I am sure that would be very exciting," Arilla replied, "and thank you very much."

As she spoke, Harry returned with two glasses of champagne in his hand and gave one to Arilla and one to Lord Rochfield before he went back to fill his own glass.

"There is no need," Lord Rochfield said in a low voice, "for me to drink to your success, for it is obvious that it will be overwhelming!"

He paused and then said:

"I can only hope you will not forget your first acquaintance in London and that I may become your friend."

"You are very . . . kind."

Lord Rochfield touched her glass with his as if they were drinking a toast, and then when Harry joined them, he said something to make them laugh.

It was half an hour before finally and quite obviously reluctantly Lord Rochfield took his leave.

Arilla was aware that he would have liked to stay to dinner, but as Harry did not invite him, she thought it would be a mistake for her to do so.

Only when Harry had seen Lord Rochfield into his carriage, which was waiting outside, and had returned to the Drawing-Room did she say:

"I am glad you came when you did! Lord Rochfield was saying some very strange things to me."

"I thought he might be!" Harry exclaimed in a hard voice.

"He apologised afterwards," Arilla went on, "and I think he would have liked to stay for dinner."

"I knew that," Harry answered, "but he is not the sort of person I would wish you to become involved with, even though he is better as a friend than as an enemy."

"Why should I not become involved with him?" Arilla enquired.

"Because, quite simply, he will not marry you!" Harry replied.

"I never thought he would," Arilla said, "but why should he not want to when he knows me better?"

"The answer to that is that Rochfield is notorious for having more love affairs than almost any man in the whole of the *Beau Monde,* and that is saying a great deal!"

Harry smiled and added:

"He has no intention whatever of having a second disastrous marriage."

"He has been married before?" Arilla exclaimed.

"Of course he has, at his age," Harry answered. "He married a perfectly charming and very suitable woman."

He frowned and added:

"She was the daughter of the Earl of Doncaster, but he treated her abominably and made her extremely unhappy."

"What did he do?" Arilla asked.

"He had a succession of mistresses, spent his time with chorus-girls, and it killed his wife. She died five years ago and I do not suppose he will ever marry again."

Harry paused and then continued:

"He has already got two sons to succeed to the title. He finds his decadent way of life, enjoying himself with woman after woman, far more attractive than the bonds of matrimony."

"He sounds horrible!" Arilla exclaimed.

"He is, and that is why you should keep away from him."

"But you were nice to him!"

"Only because I suddenly thought it would be a mistake to give him any ground for making trouble for you."

"How could he do that?"

Harry shrugged his shoulders.

"Do not let us talk about him. It is a waste of time, and time is something with which we cannot afford to be extravagant."

"I agree with you," Arilla said, "and, quite frankly, I have no wish to meet Lord Rochfield again!"

There was a little tremor in her voice as she thought of the strange things he had said to her, and the way in which he had looked at her which had made her very uncomfortable.

"Then forget him!" Harry said. "If he invites you to go

anywhere with him, just refuse! Or rather, when the occasion arises, I will tell you what to do."

"He asked me, while you were getting the champagne, if I would go driving with him in the Park, and if we would both dine with him one evening."

Harry laughed.

"Playing it cautiously, is he? It is not surprising, after he took you for a . . ."

He stopped speaking.

"A 'substitute' for Mimi, whatever that might mean," Arilla finished.

"Damn his impertinence!" Harry exclaimed angrily. "He must have realised you were a lady!"

"I think he thought until you arrived that I was somebody quite different."

Harry made a sound of exasperation.

"The whole thing was a mistake which should never have happened. I will tell the parlour-maid to make sure that no one is admitted to the house whom we do not expect."

"I suppose she thought we had invited him here," Arilla said.

"Yes, that is probably the case," Harry agreed hastily, "but it is something which must not happen again."

They went in to dinner and Harry made himself so amusing and charming that Arilla knew he was trying to reassure her after she had been upset by Lord Rochfield.

Because it was so exciting to be eating such delicious food and dining with Harry, she put Lord Rochfield out of her mind and enjoyed herself.

When the meal was finished Harry said:

"I am going to send you to bed early for the simple reason that there is a great deal for you to do tomorrow and I want you to look your best in the evening."

He paused and then went on:

"It is very important that the Countess of Jersey should accept you."

Harry hesitated and then continued:

"That is another reason why I did not want Rochfield making trouble or thinking it strange that you should be living alone in London."

"Is it strange?" Arilla asked.

"I suppose, if we were strictly conventional, you should have a companion or an older woman of some sort with you," Harry answered.

"But," he added, "I am hoping, because I am your cousin and there is no doubt of that, it will be accepted that you are living in a respectable part of the City with a number of servants."

He laughed as he said:

"And therefore no one will throw stones!"

"If I have to have a chaperone, I might as well be a *débutante*," Arilla said.

"You must be aware that in that case you would not meet half as many important people as you will as an attractive, rich widow," Harry replied.

"You mean the people to whom you introduce me will not be interested in young girls?"

"Certainly not! Most men find them a problem and a bore."

Harry hesitated and then went on:

"The only thing you have to be careful about is where men like Rochfield are concerned, who would make love to you for a very different reason than because they intend to offer you a wedding-ring."

"What reason?" Arilla enquired.

Harry debated whether he should tell her the truth, but thought it would be a mistake, and it might spoil her.

He was well aware that her innocence and the aura of purity

44

which he recognised because it was so rare was very attractive.

He thought, too, it would protect her almost more effectively than he could do.

At the same time, in her new clothes she was so lovely that he could understand why Rochfield had left the house so reluctantly.

He thought a great many men would feel the same in the future.

"I have to be very careful to see that she meets the right type," Harry told himself, "for God knows, now I come to think of it, there are far too many 'Rochfields' about!"

The thought made him frown, and Arilla said anxiously:

"You are looking cross, Harry. Have I said or done anything wrong?"

"No, of course not!" he replied. "The race begins in earnest tomorrow, so go to bed, my pretty little cousin, and think that you are off to a good start."

He smiled and added:

"Now you are over the first fence, the others will not seem so hard."

Arilla laughed and it seemed to ring out round the room.

"The first fence is really the Countess of Jersey," she said. "What I have just avoided is a rather unpleasant 'ditch' in the shape of Lord Rochfield."

"There are plenty of those, so go warily!" Harry warned.

"I shall hold on to your coat-tails and follow your lead!" Arilla promised. "Oh, Harry, this is exciting, is it not?"

"It is!" he agreed. "And whatever happens, Arilla, we will have a good run for our money!"

chapter three

Looking around the magnificent reception room with its crystal chandeliers, French furniture, Aubusson carpet, and painted ceiling, Arilla wished that her mother could see her.

She had known when Harry arrived to collect her that he approved of her appearance.

Looking in her mirror, she had thought the new gown had transformed her, and she was no longer herself but a puppet manipulated by Liza and Harry.

Her gauze dress, even with its flowers, laces, and frills round the hem, was not at all overpowering and somehow personified the arrival of Spring.

She might have been Persephone coming back from Hades into the sunshine.

She had been well aware that Harry would be critical and, as he watched her cross the room towards him, she felt a little flicker of fear in case he would after all find her dull and unattractive.

Then as he smiled she knew that everything was all right.

"I look as you wanted me to look?" she asked eagerly.

"Liza has done a good job." he replied.

They walked into the hall and he placed her scarf, which matched her gown, over her shoulders.

Then they stepped into a very comfortable carriage that was waiting outside.

It was different from the one Arilla had seen before, and she knew once again that Harry must have borrowed it, but she was too tactful to ask the question.

She realised it must be very humiliating for him to have nothing of his own, but to have to rely on the generosity of his friends.

Fortunately, they were obviously extremely open-handed where he was concerned.

But, knowing Harry so well, she knew that he wanted to be his own master.

He wanted to be able to afford to live in the style he enjoyed.

Because he was very sensitive, Arilla was sure that every day he encountered pin-pricks and uncomfortable moments when he felt, without anybody intending to hurt him, that he was degraded.

When they arrived at the Countess of Jersey's house, Arilla felt frightened, not so much for herself, but in case she and Harry were making a mistake and he would be blamed for it.

He had told her a little about the Countess and how important she was socially.

But he had in fact kept silent on the whole story of the redoubtable and, in many ways, extraordinary women who had played such a large part in the life of Prince Regent.

Harry thought a little wryly that Arilla would be shocked to hear it.

She would never understand how it was that Frances Jersey had broken up the happiness which the Prince of Wales, as he was then, enjoyed with Mrs. Fitzherbert.

The mother to two sons and seven daughters, some of whom had already provided her with grandchildren, the Countess was nine years older than the Prince. Yet she was a woman of remarkable and mature charm and undeniable beauty.

By the time Harry was old enough to listen to his father and his contemporaries talking about Frances Jersey, he had been aware that they all spoke of her fascination and seductiveness.

Because he was discerning and intelligent where people were concerned, he thought that when she practiced her allurements with the experience of an ambitious and rather heartless woman, it was not surprising that the Prince was captivated.

His father had however said:

"The Prince did not find it easy to live without Mrs. Fitzherbert. Quite frankly, he wanted both women at once, but finally, through sheer perseverance, the Countess won."

He paused, then said bitterly:

"If you want the truth, by the time you joined the Life Guards, the Prince was aware of all the wickedness, determination, and tricks of that infernal Jezebel!"

It was inevitable that after hearing so much about the Countess of Jersey, Harry should have been interested in her.

When the war was over and he came to London, he was determined to meet her.

When he did, he found her, even now that she was much older, still a seductive, sensual woman.

Because Harry was so handsome and had beautiful manners, the Countess had taken him up.

She had undoubtedly helped to make him the social success that he was.

He came from an old and distinguished family.

Nevertheless, at first, it had been of inestimable benefit to be under the patronage of someone so important, who knew everybody.

The Countess introduced Harry to the right people.

In return she expected him to dance attendance on her. To add glamour and intelligence to her special Court of attractive and intelligent people who were the envy of those who were not included in her magic circle.

She was at first furious when Harry was taken up by the Prince Regent. Because she wanted everyone around her to glitter socially as she did, she told him to make the most of the Royal favour.

"He will drop you when it suits him," she said. "He will be jealous if you do not constantly flatter him and fall in obsequiously with all his wishes, and if you were rich, he would make you pay for the privilege of knowing him!"

Harry laughed.

The Countess's sharp wit always amused him. He knew that the last threat was pointless, as he had nothing to give anyone, not even His Royal Highness.

In taking Arilla to see the Countess of Jersey he was gambling on using his instinct rather than his logic.

There was always the danger that the Countess, who was vividly aware of her own fading looks and the creeping of old age, might be jealous.

She might therefore dislike anyone so exquisite and deliberately try to hurt Arilla rather than help her.

However, he knew this was a chance he had to take. He was counting on the hope that, since Arilla looked so young, despite the wedding-ring she wore on her third finger, the Countess would feel protective rather than aggressive.

He did not say any of this to Arilla, knowing it would make her feel nervous.

He was sure she was completely unaware that one of her

great assets was that she was completely unselfconscious and, like few other women in Society, absolutely natural.

Looking at the Countess, Arilla appreciated that although she was old, in fact older than she had expected her to be, she was still beautiful.

When she smiled she had a definite charm that was irresistible.

After they had been announced, Harry led the way to where the Countess was sitting in a high-backed chair that looked almost like a throne.

She had several distinguished men grouped around her, all listening attentively to what she had to say.

As Harry reached her, she held out her hand, and as he bent and kissed it, she said:

"You are looking more handsome than ever, and I suppose that is how you beguiled me into meeting your cousin, if that is what she really is."

"How can you suggest I meant to lie to Your Ladyship?" Harry asked. But his eyes were twinkling, and almost despite herself the Countess laughed.

"You would do anything that suits you to gain your own ends!" she retorted. "But let me look at the young woman."

"Here she is," Harry said, indicating Arilla, who was standing behind him. "Lady Lindsey—the Countess of Jersey!"

Arilla made a graceful curtsy and the Countess said:

"I understand you are a widow. Well, so am I, and I can assure you that if we poor women want any freedom in our lives, we should contrive to be born both a widow and an orphan!"

There was much laughter at this sally, and the Countess went on:

"Looking as you do, it is doubtful if you will remain in

51

your enviable state for long, especially if, as your cousin informs me, your husband has left you a fortune."

Quite naturally Arilla looked shy and Harry said:

"You are embarrassing my cousin, and if she does marry again, she is determined she will be loved for herself."

"I do not suppose that will be very difficult," the Countess exclaimed, "and I am sure there will be a lot of applicants for the position."

"That is what I hope you will be kind enough to provide," Harry said daringly.

Just for a moment the Countess looked surprised, then she laughed and said:

"You were always audacious, you naughty boy! But perhaps that is why you amuse me."

She looked round at the gentlemen beside her and asked:

"Who do you suggest I introduce to this charming lady, providing her at the same time with a good reference—and I mean good!"

All the men began to talk at once. Arilla, feeling more embarrassed than ever, moved a little closer to Harry as if for protection.

He understood and gave her a reassuring smile. Then as they were interrupted by some new arrivals, he managed to say in a voice that only she could hear:

"Do not worry, you are accepted, and now everything will be plain sailing."

Arilla could not imagine how that could be, but as the Reception-Room began to fill up, the Countess introduced her to one distinguished-looking gentleman after another.

She had something witty or caustic to say about each of them.

Since Harry, hovering in the background, was obviously pleased, Arilla felt that was all that mattered.

Then just as she was conversing with a Peer who was

telling pompously of the speech he had made that afternoon in the House of Lords, she heard the Butler announce:

"Lord Rochfield, M'lady!"

Arilla started and thought that she had no wish to meet His Lordship again, and it was extremely unfortunate that he should be here to-night.

At the same time, she was aware that the Countess was greeting him with delight.

He glanced round the room, and although she quickly turned her head aside, he recognised her, and a few minutes later she heard the Countess say:

"I think, Lady Lindsey, you have met Lord Rochfield before. However, he insists on being introduced to you formally for reasons that he will not reveal to me."

"What I am hoping," Lord Rochfield said, "is that we can start our new acquaintance with no misunderstandings."

Arilla dropped him a small curtsy.

Then as she saw his dark eyes looking at her boldly in the same impertinent way he had done yesterday, she knew she positively disliked him.

There was something about him that was vaguely frightening.

She remembered only too well that Harry had warned her that she must not waste her time with him.

It was something she had in any case no wish to do, and as the Countess turned aside to greet a new arrival and she was aware that Lord Rochfield had drawn closer to her, she said a little incoherently:

"Please forgive me . . . but there is . . . someone I . . . must speak to."

This was, of course, Harry, for she knew nobody else in the room. Before Lord Rochfield could prevent her, she slipped away from him to join Harry where he was talking to an elderly Statesman.

53

He seemed a little surprised as she came to his side, and the Statesman, realising they were interrupted, moved tactfully away.

Arilla said in a low voice.

"Lord Rochfield is . . . here."

"I know," Harry replied. "Be polite, but avoid him as much as possible."

"I will try," Arilla said, "but I do not like him."

"At the same time," Harry said in a low voice, "he might make trouble, so try not to antagonise him."

It seemed to Arilla impossible to fulfill both instructions.

She was going to make a joke about it when Lord Rochfield reached them, saying in a very genial manner:

"Good-evening Vernon! I had hoped to see you today in Whites. I wanted to ask you when you could bring this charming young lady to dine with me."

He smiled at Arilla and then continued:

"I want to give a dinner-party for her, and I thought I might invite His Royal Highness, to whom I certainly owe a dinner, if not several of them."

Harry laughed.

"That might be said of all of us. But there is nothing the Prince enjoys more than being host at his own table."

"That may be," Lord Rochfield agreed, "and as for my part, I wish to be host to your lovely relative. As the party will be for her, tell me when you will both come, and after that the other guests will fall into place."

Arilla longed to say she had no wish to dine with Lord Rochfield, but tried to persuade herself she was being very foolish.

After all, he would not be the only man present, and if he was willing to play host to the Prince Regent, it was obvious that there would be other distinguished gentlemen present on whom she could focus her attention.

She was aware that Harry was thinking exactly the same thing, and as if he knew they must accept the inevitable, he said:

"You are extremely kind, My Lord, and I am sure that Lady Lindsey and I would enjoy your hospitality. We are rather heavily booked, but shall we say next Wednesday?"

"Perfect!" Lord Rochfield said. "I will see to it that Lady Lindsey enjoys herself, and who could not enjoy being in the company of one who is so beautiful?"

The words came very glibly and far too easily to be sincere, Arilla thought.

At the same time, his eyes flickered over her as they had done the night before.

Again she felt uncomfortably conscious that the *décolletage* of her gown was too low, and that the silk slip under her gauze gown revealed every curve of her figure.

To know he was looking at her made her feel shy.

Although she was so innocent, she knew it was not the way a gentleman should look at a lady whom he respected.

"He is quite odious and is behaving abominably," she told herself.

At that moment the Countess touched Harry on the arm with her fan and said:

"The Princess de Lieven has just arrived. Make a fuss of her, like a good boy, otherwise she will be spitting at us like the serpent she is!"

Arilla heard Harry give a little laugh before, to her dismay, he moved away obediently towards the Princess de Lieven, who she knew was the wife of the Russian Ambassador.

She wanted to follow him, but Lord Rochfield, taking her by the arm, moved her to a far corner of the room, where there was an empty sofa.

"Now I want you to tell me about yourself," he said. "You are so lovely that I cannot believe that even in the country, where you have been hiding, your beauty has not been extolled by the birds and the breeze."

"You are very poetical, My Lord," Arilla said, but she did not make it sound like a compliment.

"Only when I am with you," he replied. "When I saw you last night, I did not think you were real."

Arilla did not answer, but turned her face aside and he said:

"You have surely forgiven me for mistaking you for a friend of Mimi's. You must admit it was understandable in the circumstances."

"As I have no idea who Mimi is," Arilla replied, "what you are saying now is, as it was last night, completely incomprehensible."

"Let us forget everything," Lord Rochfield said quickly, "except that I find you beautiful, entrancing, and, quite frankly, my lovely lady, I have fallen in love!"

"I am sure that is . . . untrue," Arilla replied, "and so you should not say such . . . things on such a very . . . short acquaintance."

Lord Rochfield laughed.

"Can you really believe that time has anything to do with it? Love can come instantaneously like a flash of lightning, and that is what happened when I first saw you."

"I should be very suspicious of an emotion based on anything so superficial as meeting somebody for a few seconds and then making up one's mind."

Arilla spoke coldly, looking across the room to see if it was possible for her to go to Harry.

To her surprise, Lord Rochfield put his hand on her arm.

"Listen to me," he said. "I am a man of my word. I want you, and I intend that you shall be mine."

He looked at her sternly as he continued:

"I will play all the games you want me to play, but in the end you will be exactly where I wish you to be, and that is in my arms!"

Because such a declaration was not what she would have expected from any man, Arilla involuntarily turned her face towards Lord Rochfield.

She was astonished to see the fire in his eyes.

She felt as if she were looking into a burning furnace.

At the same time, his fingers tightened on her arm as if he intended to draw her closer and it would be impossible to escape.

A feeling of panic swept over her.

She wanted to jump to her feet and run away from him out of the room—anywhere—so long as she could avoid him.

Then the self-control she had exercised since she was a child came to her rescue.

"Now I am quite certain, My Lord," she said, "that you are breaking the . . . proprieties in speaking to me in . . . such a manner."

She glared at him before she continued:

"As it is . . . something to . . . which I have no . . . wish to listen, I hope you will understand why I am now . . . leaving you."

She rose determinedly as she spoke, and although he would have held her by the arm, he realised that to do so would create a scene.

As she walked away, slowly and with what she hoped was dignity, she heard him laugh quietly.

It was as if he were amused by what had happened, and at the same time intrigued.

Once again she went to Harry's side to stand listening, and to realise how skilfully and amusingly he was coping with the Princess.

He finished what he was saying and was just turning, Arilla knew, to introduce her, when a man who was beside them took the Princess's hand in his and started to talk to her in Russian.

57

"What is the matter?" Harry asked, rather sharply Arilla thought.

"His Lordship . . . frightens me," she answered. "C-can we . . . go?"

"Good God, no!" Harry replied. "Supper will be served in a few minutes, and it would be an insult to leave before midnight."

Arilla looked unhappy, and he said, still in the sharp voice he had used before:

"For Heaven's sake, remember you are not an unfledged *débutante,* but a married woman who would be able to cope with men like Rochfield."

"I . . . I will try, but it is . . . not easy."

"Nothing is easy," Harry replied, "but it is all part of the fun. Let me introduce you to a friend of mine."

He reached out as he spoke to touch the arm of a man of about his own age who was passing down the room.

"Charles," he said, "there is somebody I want you to meet."

"Hello, Harry!" the friend exclaimed. "I thought I should very likely see you here!"

Then he saw Arilla, and it was immediately obvious that he was eager to be introduced to her.

"Sir Charles Ledger—my cousin, Lady Lindsey," Harry said.

"Why have I never heard that Harry had such an entrancing cousin," Sir Charles asked. "Every relative he has introduced me to so far has been as dull as ditch-water and plain as a pike-staff!"

Arilla laughed.

"Thank you for the compliment, and I am afraid that what you have said is only too true of all our relatives!"

"And mine too!" Sir Charles said ruefully. "But then, my father always said that however much the odds are against you, a Queen must turn up sooner or later!"

He paused to smile at Arilla before he went on:

"That is certainly true where you, Lady Lindsey, are concerned!"

"Paris has indeed given you a polish, old boy!" Harry remarked. "I have never known you so glib as you are now!"

"There is quite a lot you can learn in Paris, one way or another," Sir Charles replied. There was an obvious innuendo behind his words.

"Charles," Harry explained to Arilla, "has been in Paris on behalf of the Secretary of State for Foreign Affairs, and it has obviously smartened him up a good deal!"

"I would love to go to Paris now the war is over," Arilla said wistfully, "but that is true of so many places in Europe which have been only names to us all these years of the war."

"Harry and I saw quite enough of the Continent as it happens, during the war," Sir Charles answered, "but things are very different now."

"That is what I have heard," Harry remarked, "but I would like to go and see for myself."

He gave a little sigh and Arilla knew it was because it was something he could not afford.

"If I were rich," she told herself, "I could do so much for Harry. It is pathetic that he should be so poor when all his friends have apparently plenty of money to throw about."

There was certainly no sign of shortage of it that evening.

They sat down to a magnificent supper at which there was every luxury to eat and such superb wines that Harry and Charles sitting either side of her kept talking about them.

"If you ask me," Sir Charles said, "Her Ladyship is trying to outvie the parties at Carlton House, or the Royal Pavilion at Brighton."

He stopped talking a moment, before he went on:

"In fact, it is what all the 'big-wigs' are intending to do now that his Royal Highness has moved in to what is a veritable Aladdin's cave."

"A very good description of it," Harry approved, "and it must have cost, as they say, a King's ransom!"

"I am not sure that I admire it all," Sir Charles said reflectively. "All that Chinese stuff is not really my taste, but I have to admit that the whole thing is very impressive and exactly the sort of background 'Prinny' should have."

"I agree with you there," Harry said.

Arilla wondered if she would ever have an opportunity of visiting Carlton House or the Royal Pavilion.

She remembered a little sadly that the Prince Regent liked only older women, if the gossips and Harry were to be believed, and Lady Hertford was a grandmother several times over.

When they went back to the Drawing-Room after supper, a String Orchestra was playing softly at the far end of the room, and it sounded very romantic.

Harry and Sir Charles soon became involved in a conversation about the races that were taking place the following day.

Arilla moved a little way from them to look at a picture that she was sure was a Rubens.

Then once again she heard Lord Rochfield's voice, saying:

"You are far more beautiful than any picture, and I want to go on looking at you to make sure I do not lose you."

Arilla had noticed that at supper he was sitting on one side of their hostess.

Because she valued Harry's advice that the Countess could be very helpful to her, she was afraid that, if she once again ran away from him, he might cause trouble.

"I am sure you are very knowledgeable about pictures," she said ingenuously, "so would you tell me about the ones in this room, which I can see are very fine."

"As I have already said, I personally would rather look at you!" Lord Rochfield said. "But let me show you a picture that it would be impossible for you not to admire. It is by Poussin."

He led her to the far end of the Drawing-Room.

There she saw that it was indeed a magnificent picture exquisitely painted, and she knew it was something she would be thrilled to own herself.

Almost as if he were aware of what she was thinking, Lord Rochfield said:

"Shall I give you a picture which will delight you, as I can see this one does, or would you rather have diamonds?"

Arilla stiffened.

She was quite certain it was wrong and insulting for a man to offer her jewellery, and she said quickly:

"Of course, you are talking hypothetically, but I think even more than pictures or jewels, if I ever had the choice, I would prefer horses."

"Then that is what you shall have!" Lord Rochfield said firmly.

Arilla gave a little cry.

"I was, of course, not speaking seriously. In fact, I actually said that I was speaking hypothetically. Naturally, My Lord, I could not possibly accept a present from you, whatever it might be."

"Why not?" Lord Rochfield enquired. "Because you come from the country you are very naïve."

He paused a moment before continuing:

"I would be surprised if there is any lady in this room who has not accepted presents, and very expensive ones, from some man who has found it an easy way to express his affection for her."

He seemed to be speaking in a voice that was really sincere, and Arilla looked at him in surprise.

"Perhaps, My Lord," she said, "in the country we have different standards of behaviour from what you have here. I have always believed that no lady should accept presents except from her husband."

Lord Rochfield gave a twisted smile before he said:

"What you are telling me is very clear—that what you want is not very expensive, but more valuable to a woman than pictures, diamonds, or horses—a wedding-ring!"

"That is not what I was actually thinking," Arilla said, "but perhaps what you say is true."

She thought as she spoke that she had been quite clever.

Harry had made it clear that Lord Rochfield was not the marrying sort. She was well aware that the Prince Regent's infatuation for older women could not end in marriage.

She could quite understand therefore why his behaviour scandalised people. She was sure her mother would have been very shocked by Lord Rochfield.

As if the conversation were finished, she lifted her face towards the Poussin again.

She was sure it was one of the loveliest pictures she would ever see, however many other houses she visited.

Then she heard Lord Rochfield say very quietly:

"So you want to be married again, my lovely one? That is certainly something we must discuss in the future."

Arilla thought she had not heard him aright.

Then, as she turned to look into his dark eyes, there was an expression in them which she did not understand but of which she felt definitely afraid.

As she was trying to think of some way by which she could leave Lord Rochfield, he had come a little closer to her and said:

"I suppose you realise that since I saw you last night I have been unable to get your face out of my mind, and all day long I have seen nothing but the beauty of your eyes and the gold in your hair."

There was a deep note in his voice which made it impossible for Arilla to look at him, fearing to see the fire in his eyes.

Because she was afraid, she felt almost as if he were hypnotising her, pulling her to him so that she could not escape.

Too late, she realised it had been a mistake to come with him to a more isolated part of the Salon. She should have stayed with the crowd, where Harry was.

"I know what you are thinking," Lord Rochfield said. "You want to run away from me, and I find it very exciting and at the same time incomprehensible. You have had a husband. Were you afraid of him?"

"That is not something I want to talk about," Arilla said.

"If he had not put a ring on your finger," Lord Rochfield went on, "I should find it hard to believe that any man has possessed you, or even that you have been kissed."

He paused but she did not reply, so he continued:

"There is something pure and untouched about you which I find so entrancing that I am caught in your spell."

There was now a passion in his voice that made Arilla feel even more frightened.

She turned to look down the room, and to her utter relief she saw Harry moving in her direction.

Only by a superhuman effort of self-control did she prevent herself from running towards him and holding on to him.

Instead, she smiled at him, and he knew from the expression in her eyes how glad she was to see him.

As he reached her he said:

"If you are really intent on riding early as you said you were on your way here, it is now possible for us to leave."

"I would like that," Arilla said quickly, "and I am actually very tired."

"I think, if the truth were known," Lord Rochfield said, "you are once again running away."

"Running away?" Harry exclaimed. "Have you been upsetting my little cousin? You must remember she comes from the country and is not used to 'Gay Lotharios' like Your Lordship."

"She has made that very clear!" Lord Rochfield replied. "But I assure you, I have no wish to upset or hurt her in any way."

"I wish I could be certain of that," Harry replied.

Now he spoke in a way it was impossible for Lord Rochfield not to understand.

"You can trust me," he said, "and I hope I may have the pleasure of calling on Lady Lindsey tomorrow."

"I have really no . . . idea what I . . . shall be . . . doing," Arilla said a little incoherently.

"We shall be very busy," Harry answered. "I have a tight programme arranged and I doubt if we could squeeze anything, however small, into it."

"That is a challenge, Vernon," Lord Rochfield said, "or would you rather make it a wager?"

"That is definitely something I cannot afford!" Harry replied. "I hope a challenge will be less expensive."

"I hope you will think so!"

The eyes of the two men met as if in deadly rivalry.

Suddenly Arilla was frightened that if Harry antagonised Lord Rochfield, it really would harm him and perhaps make things more difficult than they were already.

She held out her hand to Lord Rochfield.

"Thank you for being so very kind in showing me this picture."

She smiled at him and continued:

"If I talked a lot of nonsense, you must put it down to the fact that I am not only tired, but also overwhelmed and bewildered by such an exciting and for me very unusual evening."

Lord Rochfield took her hand in his and raised it not at all perfunctorily to his lips.

Arilla felt his lips on her bare skin.

It gave her the feeling that she was being touched by a reptile, something so frightening and dangerous that she wanted to scream.

Then with a smile that was worthy of any actress however famous at Drury Lane, she said:

"Goodnight, My Lord, and thank you again."

She turned away, then having said goodnight to the Countess, she and Harry left.

Only as the borrowed carriage left behind the link men with their lighted torches did Harry say angrily:

"Now tell me what that swine said to make you look so frightened!"

chapter four

Arilla deliberately chose the gown she liked the least, hoping that Lord Rochfield would think it did not become her.

She had almost forgotten that they were to dine with him.

Then, as she and Harry were leaving a smart and enjoyable party, she heard the voice which she so much disliked saying:

"I shall see you tomorrow evening, lovely lady."

She started, then, realising who had spoken, she managed with difficulty before walking quickly away to the carriage which was waiting for them to say politely;

"Yes, of course. Harry and I are looking forward to it."

Now she felt depressed and thought the evening was certain to be uncomfortable, even though Harry would be there to protect her.

Rose, the maid who was helping her to dress, said as she finished fastening her gown at the back:

"You look lovely, M'Lady, you do really, an' it's a pleasure to see you!"

"Thank you," Arilla replied, "but I am sure Miss Mimi looks much lovelier when she goes out."

This was really a bow at a venture because she had found it impossible to talk about the owner of the house to Harry.

She also had the feeling that the servants in the house were reluctant to mention her.

It seemed strange, because nothing could be more feminine or more attractive than the bedroom in which she was sleeping.

Harry had said that the furniture and pictures belonged to Lord Barlow.

But there were many other things in the house which were obviously feminine and would never have been thought of by a man.

There was a little pause before Rose said:

"Yes, of course, M'Lady, but that's different."

Then as Arilla was about to continue the conversation, Rose said:

"What jewelry are you going to wear, M'Lady, if I may ask?"

Arilla looked at her reflection in the mirror and was aware that without jewels there seemed to be a big expanse of her white skin.

She was sure that Lord Rochfield would once again make her feel that her *décolletage* was too low.

She then asked herself for the first time why Harry had not borrowed some jewels for her to wear.

The first night when they were going out to dinner he had, when she came downstairs, opened a box that was lying on one of the small tables in the Drawing-Room, saying:

"I have brought a very important addition to your appearance as a rich widow."

"What is that?" Arilla enquired.

"Diamonds!" Harry replied briefly.

Arilla looked at him in surprise and he opened the box, revealing a large and very ornate diamond necklace.

Arilla had gasped.

"Harry! Where did you get it?"

"I borrowed it," he explained, "and for God's sake do not lose it! If you do, I could certainly never afford to replace it!"

"It is very . . . grand!" Arilla said tentatively.

As it happened, she thought it was a little over-powering and almost vulgar.

But she understood that if she was to appear to be as rich as Harry had described her to be, she would certainly, as a married woman be wearing jewels.

It was something she had forgotten herself.

Then when they arrived at the Countess of Jersey's she was aware that quite a number of people to whom she was introduced stared as much at her necklace as they did at her face.

After that, for every party, Harry had provided her with jewelry of some sort.

Last night he had brought her a necklace which she had definitely thought was gaudy and in bad taste.

She put it on as he expected her to do, but when he had looked at her, he said:

"Take that thing off! I thought it was all wrong, but as I had asked a friend to be generous enough to lend me something, I could hardly find fault with her choice."

"It is very kind," Arilla said. "At the same time, I am glad you do not like it."

Instead, Harry had suggested that she wear a band of velvet ribbon round her neck and attached to it a single white orchid.

It made Arilla look very Spring-like and although she did not realise it, even lovelier than before.

It had gained the approval of some of the older ladies at the party, for Harry had overheard one of them saying:

"The rich widow is certainly unassuming and behaves in a manner I find discreet and dignified."

"I agree with you," another Dowager had replied, "and I like the way she does not flaunt her jewels. I shall certainly include her on my visiting-list."

When Harry had repeated the conversation to Arilla she had laughed.

Now she was thinking that this evening he would expect her to repeat her success by wearing flowers rather than the jewels she did not possess.

She sent Rose downstairs to try to find amongst the baskets and bouquets of flowers which had been arriving all day a small blossom which would look pretty round her neck.

Unfortunately the flowers which Rose had brought back did not look right.

Finally Arilla had tied a piece of pink velvet ribbon round her neck and left it unadorned.

"That looks very pretty, M'Lady," Rose said approvingly.

"I wish I had something to put to the front of it," Arilla said more to herself than to the maid.

"It looks just right th' way it is," Rose insisted, "and I'm sure Mr. Harry, as us calls him, 'll say so too."

"I hope so," Arilla murmured.

Then on an impulse she asked:

"You say you call Mr. Vernon 'Mr. Harry.' Does he come here very often?"

"Oh, yes, M'Lady," Rose answered. "Miss Mimi dotes on him, as you might say, and it's a pity 'e can't afford—"

She stopped suddenly, as if she were saying something indiscreet, and added a little lamely:

"But His Lordship's very generous, an' we're all very 'appy to be working for him."

"But he does not live here?" Arilla questioned.

She remembered that when she had driven through Berkeley Square with Harry, he had pointed out Brandon House and she had thought it very impressive.

"Oh, no, M'Lady!" Rose said. "'Is Lordship only comes when he can, so to speak, but there's other gentlemen, although us finds Mr. Harry the nicest of 'em all."

It all seemed puzzling to Arilla, but she did not wish to ask any more questions.

She could only wonder why nobody could explain what exactly was the position Miss Mimi had in Lord Brandon's life.

Although she had asked Harry several times in what Theatre Miss Mimi was appearing, his answer had been vague, and he had merely said:

"She is 'resting' at the moment, and that is why she has been able to go to Paris with His Lordship."

It also made it easy, Arilla thought, for Harry to rent the house without paying anything for it.

As well as to use, although that, too, seemed strange, a carriage and horses from Lord Brandon's stable.

She was, however, content to leave everything in Harry's hands and she thought that he would soon be arriving to collect her.

She also thought how much easier it would be if, instead of having to go to dinner with Lord Rochfield, they could dine alone downstairs.

Now she thought about it, she had seen very little of Harry, except in the company of other people.

Although he told her what to wear and inspected her carefully before he took her anywhere, there was always a large party, a Ball, or an Assembly waiting for them.

Once they were there, she knew there was no chance of talking to him and she must concentrate on the gentlemen to whom she was introduced.

She found it impossible not to think each time an introduction was made that this might be the man she would have to marry.

Last night, although it seemed incredible after such a short time, she had received her first proposal of marriage.

It had come from a young Peer whom she had met twice before at other dinner-parties.

He had been seated next to her and although there were over thirty other guests he had concentrated on her.

It was in such a way that she felt was rather rude to the lady on his other side and also somewhat embarrassing.

After dinner there had been dancing.

The Peer had insisted on taking her from the Ball-Room into a room next to it. The pretext was that he wanted to show her a picture he thought she would admire.

When they had entered the room it was empty, and to her surprise he shut the door, saying:

"At last I have managed to be with you alone, and I must seize this opportunity of asking you if you will do me the honour of becoming my wife."

Arilla had stared at him in sheer astonishment.

This was something she had not expected. She had certainly not thought any proposal of marriage would be so banal or so hasty.

For one moment she thought it might be a joke, then as she looked up at him, her eyes wide with surprise, he said:

"Marry me, please marry me! I swear I will make you happy, and there are so many things that we could do together on my estate."

As he spoke he took her hand in his and because she had not put on her gloves after dinner he covered it with kisses.

His lips, somehow hard and somehow urgent, made her feel uncomfortable.

"I am . . . very sorry . . ." she began in a rather tremulous voice. To her relief the door opened and several other people came into the room.

They made it easy for her to escape by insisting on returning to the Ball-Room, and once they were there, she hurried to Harry's side.

He was talking to a very beautiful woman whom he had sat next to at dinner and who Arilla had thought was obviously very enamoured of him.

She had looked at him in a manner which appeared to reveal her feelings very clearly.

She was now standing with her face raised to his, saying something very intimate.

Her hand, flashing with a large diamond ring, was on Harry's arm.

As Arilla came up beside him he smiled at her before he said:

"So here you are! I was hoping I would have the opportunity of introducing you to one of my oldest and of course dearest friends—the Marchioness of Westbury."

The Marchioness, however, did not seem at all pleased by Arilla's intervention. She merely nodded to her somewhat disdainfully before she said:

"Do not forget, Harry. I shall expect you and shall be very angry if you do not turn up."

"How could you be unkind to me?" Harry asked.

There was a mocking note in his voice, and as the Marchioness turned away, he looked at Arilla with a frown on his forehead.

Then he asked in a voice that only she could hear:

"What has upset you?"

"I cannot . . . tell you . . . here," Arilla replied, afraid that the people near them would hear what she had to say.

"Then come and dance," Harry said, putting his arm around her and drawing her towards the dance-floor.

The Band was playing a soft, sentimental Waltz which had just been introduced to London by the Princess de Lieven.

The Dowagers were already saying it was improper.

Questioning whether it was correct for a young girl, or an older woman for that matter, to be dancing so close to a man.

Arilla had already found that Harry was a superb dancer, and as they moved over the polished floor, she said in a rather nervous little voice:

"The Earl of Fladbury . . . has just . . . proposed to me!"

As she spoke, she was terrified in case Harry should say she ought to marry him.

To her surprise Harry merely laughed and it was a very genuine sound.

She looked up at him, as if for explanation, and he said:

"I thought that was what Fladbury intended, and I meant to warn you."

"To warn . . . me?"

"He is looking for a rich wife!"

Arilla gave a little sigh of relief.

As if he knew what she was feeling, Harry said:

"Do not worry about Fladbury. He has pursued every heiress for the last two years and every month he gets deeper and deeper into debt."

"I . . . I was . . . afraid," Arilla admitted in a whisper.

"That you would have to marry him?" Harry asked. "That is one thing you will never have to do. He is in the hands of the Usurers and completely irresponsible. I would not wish him on my worst enemy!"

The way he spoke made Arilla laugh again.

Suddenly, as Harry swung her around, the party seemed amusing and the lights from the chandeliers more brilliant than they had been previously.

* * *

Now Arilla was thinking that however difficult, and perhaps boring, the party would be, at least she would not be troubled by a proposal of marriage from Lord Rochfield.

She disliked both the way he spoke to her and the man himself. In a crowd, she could avoid him by blending in.

She only hoped that his guests would be more attractive than he was and that she and Harry would not have to stay too late.

Rose went to the wardrobe to bring her a wrap to cover her gown.

It was very pretty and made of pale blue velvet which went with most of her gowns and was trimmed with white maribou.

This, as Liza had told her, was all the fashion at the moment.

She put it loosely round her shoulders.

As Arilla took a last look at herself in the mirror there was a knock on the bedroom door.

Rose opened it and the parlour-maid said:

"The carriage be here, M'Lady, but th' footman says as how Mr. Vernon's been delayed and 'll meet you at 'Is Lordship's house."

Arilla felt a little pang of disappointment.

One thing she always enjoyed was being alone with Harry when he came to take her to wherever they were going.

She could then talk to him on the way and on the return journey without having to keep up the pretence of being a rich widow.

She wondered what was making him late and thought it was probably the Marchioness of Westbury, or somebody like her.

She was well aware how sought-after Harry was by the beautiful women they met night after night wherever they went.

Arilla realised that they were much older than she was. Soophisticated, witty, and so beautiful that it was not surprising that Harry seemed very familiar with them.

They certainly did not hide their feelings about him.

"He must find it a nuisance having to look . . . after me," she thought.

The carriage was a very large and comfortable one which she had not seen before and she wondered from whom Harry had borrowed it.

The horses were certainly well-bred, and as soon as the carriage-door closed, they set off at a sharp pace towards the West End.

Arilla hoped that Harry would be there when she arrived.

She thought, a little late, that it might have been wiser to have made sure of it.

She could have kept the carriage waiting instead of leaving the minute it arrived.

But there was nothing she could do about it now, except hope there would be plenty of other guests there already.

They would make it impossible for their host to talk to her in the intimate manner that she most disliked.

She had not told Harry how nervous Lord Rochfield made her because she thought he would think it foolish.

He had made it very clear that it would be a mistake to have him as an enemy.

She knew therefore it would not help matters if she deliberately tried to set Harry against him.

At the same time, there was something about His Lordship which frightened her.

She felt he was sly and she wanted to avoid him at all costs.

It did not take more than twenty minutes for the carriage to reach Rochfield House in Piccadilly.

Not far from the magnificent house at Hyde Park Corner which had just been built for the Duke of Wellington, Rochfield House faced onto Green Park.

The house stood back a little from Piccadilly itself and its entrance was very impressive with double gates surmounted by heraldic unicorns.

Arilla suspected these were incorporated in Lord Rochfield's coat of arms.

A red carpet had been laid over the steps leading up to the front door, and a Butler and four footmen were waiting in the marble hall.

One of the footmen took Arilla's velvet wrap from her and the Butler then led her up a curved stairway to the First Floor.

He did not stop, however, at what Arilla thought would be the Drawing-Room at the top of the stairs, but went on down a wide corridor.

It was lit by candles in golden sconces and hung with some impressive pictures.

At any other time she would have been interested both in the pictures and in the very fine pieces of French furniture which stood beneath them.

But she was worried because no other guests seemed to have arrived and she thought she was too early.

Once again she was wishing she had been sensible enough to keep the carriage waiting and arrive very much later.

She had become aware at other parties that there was always a distinguished and very lovely Beauty who arrived last, making a deliberately theatrical entrance after everybody else was there.

"That is what I should have done," Arilla told herself. "How can I have been so foolish, as I was alone, not to have waited and made sure that Harry would get here first?"

The Butler opened a door and announced:

"Lady Lindsey, M'Lord!"

As she entered the room, Arilla realised with a little construction of her heart that there was no one there except for Lord Rochfield.

He was standing in front of a marble fireplace which was flanked by two Chinese bowls filled with Madonna lilies.

Arilla was aware that he deliberately did not move to greet her but waited for her to come to him.

She moved more slowly than she would normally have done because she was frightened.

She had no idea that her eyes not only filled her small face, but also reflected her feelings.

Only when she was within a few feet of Lord Rochfield did she say:

"I am . . . afraid . . . My Lord . . . that I am . . . a little early and . . . my cousin, as he has been delayed . . . has sent me a message to say that he will . . . meet me here."

"I am sure Vernon has a very good reason for being late," Lord Rochfield replied, and Arilla hated him for the obvious innuendo behind the words. "But you are here, and that is all that matters."

He took her hand in his and raised it to his lips and at his touch she felt herself shiver.

A footman had followed her into the room, carrying two glasses of champagne on a tray.

He offered one to Arilla, which she accepted, then went to Lord Rochfield with the other.

As he took it Lord Rochfield said:

"Tonight I must drink a very special toast because this is the first time you have visited my house and I hope you will admire it."

"I see you have some very fine pictures," Arilla remarked, thinking that was a safe subject for discussion.

"Some of them are of goddesses," he replied, "but none of them are as beautiful or as alluring as you!"

His eyes, as he spoke, were flickering over her.

He made her feel as if her gown were both transparent and too low in the front.

Without meaning to, she looked towards the door, wondering frantically why Harry had not arrived and where the other guests were.

To her relief, almost as if she compelled it to do so, the door opened, but it was not Harry who appeared, but the Butler.

He did not announce anyone, but walked across the room to stand near to Lord Rochfield.

"A messenger has just arrived from Mr. Vernon, M'Lord, to say he hopes Your Lordship will accept his apologies, but unfortunately owing to circumstances over which he has no control, he's unable to dine with Your Lordship this evening."

"Thank you," Lord Rochfield said.

The Butler left the room and Arilla said quickly:

"What do you think can have happened? How can Harry possibly have thrown over your invitation at the last minute?"

Lord Rochfield smiled knowingly.

"That is very easily explainable. The 'circumstances' over which your cousin has no control could be the Prince Regent, or perhaps he had had a more attractive invitation from the beautiful Marchioness."

"But that . . . would be very . . . rude," Arilla said in a low voice.

"I can only accept it as a gift from the gods," Lord Rochfield answered, "that by what seems a miracle I have you all to myself."

Arilla drew in her breath.

"But . . . what about . . . the . . . rest of the . . . party?" she managed to ask.

"Because I wanted to talk to you, lovely lady," he replied, "I had no intention of having your attention, or mine, diverted by other guests, who would have only been an encumbrance."

"D-do you mean . . . we are alone?"

"What could be more entrancing?" Lord Rochfield questioned. "And may I say I have been looking forward to this evening, and I feel sure I shall not be disappointed!"

There was an alarming forcefulness about the way he spoke.

She knew that she dare not look at him for fear of what she would see in his eyes.

As she tried frantically to think of something she could say, some way by which she could protect herself, dinner was announced.

Lord Rochfield offered her his arm and there was nothing she could do but set her fingers very lightly upon it and allow him to escort her from the room into the wide passage outside.

She had expected that they would go down the stairs, assuming that, as was usual, the Dining-Room would be situated on the Ground Floor.

Instead, he led her farther along the corridor to where a footman stood holding open a door at what seemed to Arilla to be almost the end of the house.

When she entered the room she found it was small and comfortably furnished with sofas and low chairs and decorated with a profusion of white flowers.

It seemed strange, but for the moment she could think of nothing except that in the centre of the room there was a table laid for two people.

It was lit by a golden candelabrum holding four candles.

She found she was not to be seated opposite her host, but beside him.

As a footman brought in the first course the Butler served the wine.

Arilla was aware that the candelabrum on the table and two

candles on what was being used as a sideboard were the only lights in the room.

She felt that the whole scene was utterly bizarre.

To be dining alone, in a Sitting-Room rather than a Dining-Room, decorated almost like a bower with nothing but white flowers, and with a man she heartily disliked.

It made her feel as if it were impossible to eat and that any food would choke her.

However, with the servants in the room she knew that she must behave circumspectly.

At the same time, she was worrying frantically how she could escape from what she knew was a dangerous situation.

As if he were aware of her feelings and wanted to soothe them, Lord Rochfield began to talk quite interestingly of his possessions and of the parties they had both attended in the last few days.

Arilla was, however, afraid to meet his eyes.

She was quite sure that when her face was averted he was looking at her in the way she most disliked.

The dinner was smaller than she might have expected, what she did manage to eat was delicious, and when it was ended, Lord Rochfield said:

"Now let us sit more comfortably on the sofa and I am going to persuade you to have a very exotic liqueur while I drink a glass of brandy."

"I want nothing more!" Arilla said quickly.

She had been aware that her glass of champagne was continually being filled, even though she took only tiny sips of it.

She was afraid that if she drank even a little, it might make her less alert to the possibility of escape from Lord Rochfield without there being an uncomfortable scene.

Because there was nothing else she could do, she got up

from the table. As the servants were quickly clearing every-thing away she said nervously:

"I think . . . as your party did not . . . materialise . . . it would be correct for me to . . . leave you and . . . return home."

Lord Rochfield laughed.

"That is something I cannot allow, and my carriage which brought you here will certainly not be waiting outside until very much later."

"Your carriage?" Arilla questioned.

"But of course!" Lord Rochfield replied. "I wanted to make sure of your arrival."

She thought it strange that Harry should have allowed Lord Rochfield to send for her, but there was nothing she could say.

Despite her refusal, the servants put a glass of what she was sure was a very potent liqueur beside her.

She ignored it, and sitting in a corner of the sofa as far away from Lord Rochfield as she could get, she said:

"I . . . I hope, my Lord . . . you will be aware of my wishes not to . . . endanger my reputation . . . by being here . . . alone with you . . . which I did not expect . . . and I would like to leave . . . now that dinner is over."

"Your reputation is quite safe with me," Lord Rochfield said, "and there is no reason for anybody to know we are alone. What happens between us will be our secret, unless, of course, you chatter, which I feel is unlikely."

He moved a little nearer to her as he spoke.

She felt herself shiver knowing it was impossible to move any farther away from him.

"I have been thinking of this all day!" Lord Rochfield said quietly. "Do you realise the flowers here and in another room we shall visit shortly are a tribute to your beauty?"

"They . . . they are lovely!" Arilla said quickly. "I am very fond of lilies."

"It seems strange that I should associate them with you, considering you are a married woman," Lord Rochfield remarked. "But there is something innocent and untouched about you."

He paused a moment, a wicked leer on his face, before he went on:

"It tells me that if I am not the first man to touch you, I shall certainly be the first to awaken you to the joys and delights of love."

The way he spoke made Arilla feel as if she were faced by a vicious serpent, and her impulse was to jump up and run away from him.

Instead, lifting her chin a little, she said:

"I . . . I do not think you should talk to me like . . . that. If you will not tell me about your possessions . . . which I can see are priceless . . . I know that I must . . . leave you."

Again Lord Rochfield laughed.

"I find you entrancing!" he said. "I know you are frightened, and yet you are being very brave in your defiance."

There was almost a caressing note in his voice as he went on:

"Shall I tell you that you attract me as no woman has been able to do for a very long time?"

He stopped speaking, and leered at her again before continuing:

"When I have taught you the first lessons of desire, you will find we can deal very well together, and very comfortably."

He put out his hand towards her as he spoke, and despite her resolution to remain calm, Arilla sprang to her feet like a frightened fawn.

She would have run towards the door, but Lord Rochfield reached out and caught her by the wrist.

"Not so fast, my dear!" he said. "I have something to

show you—something which will explain better than any words what I want."

"Let me go!"

With a superhuman effort Arilla managed to keep her voice low and to speak with what she hoped would sound like the word of command.

Holding on to her, Lord Rochfield rose to his feet.

Instead of putting his arms round her as she expected, he moved, still holding her by the wrist, towards a door she had not noticed.

It stood in a corner near a curtained window and obviously communicated with another room.

He pulled it open, and once again she was aware of great bowls of lilies and the fragrance of them which filled the air.

Then she saw a huge canopied bed with the sheets turned back to reveal the lace-edged pillows.

It was visible in the light of two small candelabra on either side of the bed.

Without speaking, Arilla stared in a bemused fashion at what lay in front of her.

Then Lord Rochfield said:

"Now you know what I want, and what I intend to have! You are mine, my beautiful, and there is no escape!"

As he spoke he put his arm around her.

It was then that Arilla realised she was caught in a trap and with a scream of terror she started to struggle with him.

It was what he must have anticipated, for he now put both his arms around her and held her against him with arms like bands of steel.

Knowing she was lost, she could only scream and scream again. . . .

* * *

Harry walked through the door of his lodgings in Half Moon Street and climbed the three flights of stairs to the top floor.

Half Moon Street contained some of the smartest lodgings available for the young Bucks who frequented St. James's.

Harry had known that although it was the fashion, it was something he could not afford.

However it was Watkins, who had looked after him when he was in the Life Guards, who had found the attic of No. 19.

It had been used for storing trunks owned by the lodgers who lived below and any furniture that was not required at the moment.

He had managed somehow to persuade the owner of the house that even a minute rent, which was all Harry could afford, would be better than nothing.

Harry had therefore been able to lease two very small attic rooms, which provided him with a bedroom and a Sitting-Room.

It was Watkins, too, who kept them clean and tidy.

He also looked after Harry's clothes so that he was, without exception, the best-dressed besides being the most handsome man in the *Beau Monde*.

"It is no use, Watkins," Harry had said when they left the Regiment. "You know I would like above all things to keep you as my valet, but I just have not the money to pay you, and that is the truth!"

"Oi knows that, Cap'ain," Watkins replied, "but jest you leave everythin' ter me."

"That is what I would like to do," Harry answered, "but it is impossible!"

"Maybe," Watkins said obstinately, "and maybe not!"

He found himself a job working at one of the stalls in the Market.

He called Harry in the mornings and gave him his breakfast, and he helped him dress in the evenings before he went out to dinner.

If Harry had a little money, which was not often, he gave it to Watkins.

When he had none, Watkins lived on what he earned in the Market and in fact spent quite a lot of it on Harry.

"I really do not know what I would do without you," Harry said often enough, and he meant it.

When he reached the top of the stairs, he was not surprised to find everything neat and tidy and ready for him.

His clothes had been laid out, and he knew it would be only a short while before Watkins would appear to get his bath ready and to help him dress.

He went into the small Sitting-Room to find letters on his desk in the window ready for him to open.

There were a number of invitations which he glanced at, and several letters addressed in flowing, feminine hands on expensive writing-paper.

Each smelt of different scents he was able to identify to each correspondent.

There was one scented with gardenias which Harry threw on one side without opening it, another of lilies-of-the-valley which made him smile, and another that had the fragrance of tuberoses brought a gleam to his eye.

He had just glanced at the clock on the mantelpiece when he heard Watkins coming to the door.

He was carrying shirts that had been washed and ironed.

They had the perfection that had been demanded by Beau Brummell before he fled to the Continent and white cravats starched to exactly the right stiffness.

"Evenin', Captain!" Watkins said cheerily.

"I was just thinking it was time I had my bath," Harry replied.

"There's no 'urry now."

"What do you mean?" Harry asked.

"A messenger turned up a short while ago afore I went t' fetch these," Watkins explained, indicating the pile of shirts and cravats, "to say that 'Er Ladyship 'as a 'eadache, and can't go out this evenin'."

"A headache?" Harry repeated in surprise. "She seemed perfectly well when I saw her at luncheontime."

They had been the guests of Lady Holland, a witty older woman who was noted for her intelligent conversation and the interesting people she entertained.

Harry had been delighted to find that Arilla could "hold her own" in a conversation that was very different from the frivolous gossip sprinkled with innuendoes typical of the other hostesses in the *Beau Monde*.

In fact, she had two of the most intelligent men in London listening to her attentively.

Having been driven back to Islington, she was still as sparkling as she had been at the luncheon-table.

As he hurriedly left her to keep an appointment with the Prince Regent at Carlton House, he had almost forgotten she would be nervous about the evening because they were dining with Lord Rochfield.

Now he thought he should have reassured her that he would look after her.

He was quite certain that her headache was just a pretence to avoid a man she disliked.

Harry was aware, however, that Lord Rochfield could be a dangerous enemy.

Although he had no liking himself for the man, he knew, because he was rich and therefore fawned on by the Social World, it would be a mistake for Arilla to antagonise him.

He was fearful that he might defame her.

Or perhaps make embarrassing enquiries about her which could prove disastrous.

It did not particularly surprise Harry that she had refused at the last minute to face the dinner-party.

He had not expected to enjoy it himself despite the fact that His Lordship was noted for providing the finest cuisine and the finest wines.

Now that Arilla had refused, it left him with nothing to do that evening.

As Harry stretched himself out in a comfortable chair, he said to Watkins:

"If that is the position, as I was late last night, I will have a quiet snooze and then I will change and go to Whites."

"Oi thought as you'd do that, Sir," Watkins said, "an' it'll give me time t'get your bath ready."

He shut the door of the Sitting-Room and Harry shut his eyes, thinking as he did so of how pretty Arilla had looked at luncheon, and what a success she was being.

"No one can say that I am not doing my best for her," he told himself, "but she should certainly expect a better proposal soon than from that fortune-hunter Fladbury!"

There was a mocking twist to his lips as he thought how horrified Fladbury would have been if Arilla had accepted him.

Only to find out later that she was as impoverished as he was.

He was still thinking, when he fell asleep, of how pretty Arilla had looked when she was laughing.

* * *

Harry was awoken by Watkins's saying:

"Yer bath's ready, Sir, and if you don't 'urry, Cap'ain, it'll be cold!"

Harry yawned, then walked into his small Bedroom.

He let Watkins help him out of his fashionably tight coat and his even tighter closely-woven champagne-coloured pantaloons that fitted like the proverbial glove.

He had taken a leisurely bath and was brushing his hair into the elegant "wind-swept" style introduced by the Prince Regent when Watkins said:

"I was jus' thinkin', Cap'ain, that the message from 'Er Ladyship an' the one for you were delivered by the same messenger."

"What do you mean—the one for me?" Harry asked.

"Well, when I comes here early to collect yer shirts, Cap'ain," Watkins said, "I was jus' comin' through the dahnstairs door when a lad says t'me:

" 'Oi've got a message for Mr. Vernon from Lady Lindsey.'

" ' 'E ain't in,' I says, 'so tell me!'

" ' 'Er Ladyship's got a 'eadache and her's sorry, but her can't go out this evenin',' th' boy says.

" 'Righto', I answers, 'I'll tell 'im.' An' he goes orf.

"Then I wonders as 'e does so wot 'e's a-doin' in the house at Islington, an' I remembers whenever we've bin there there weren't no men-servants about."

"Go on!" Harry prompted.

"Well, I goes upstairs to fetch your shirts," Watkins continued, "tidies up a bit, then about half-an-hour later when I gets down to the bottom of the stairs, I remembers I ain't got yer cravats, so up I goes again an' when I comes dahn there's the same lad.

" 'Hello,' I says, 'wot is it now?'

" ' 'Nother message for Mr. Vernon,' 'e says.

" 'Wot is it this time?' I enquires.

" 'The message be ter say that Lord Rochfield be sorry, but th' dinner for tonight be cancelled!'

" 'E says it quick-like," Watkins said, "as if he were quotin' wot 'e'd bin taught. Then 'e turns an' 'urries orf."

Harry turned round from the dressing-table, and he was frowning.

"There is something wrong about this!" he said sharply. "Give me my coat!"

Watkins helped him into his evening-coat.

"I knows yer'd worret yourself, Cap'ain," he said, "but I thinks 'twas strange!"

"Too damned strange for my liking!" Harry said.

He took the tall hat that Watkins held out to him, then put it down on a chair.

"If I want it, I will come back for it later."

Then before Watkins could expostulate, Harry had run down the stairs and out through the front door.

It took him only a few minutes to reach the Mews at the back of the houses in Piccadilly.

There was a large stable in the mews behind the walls of the garden of Rochfield House.

Harry walked into the first stall he came to, to find a coachman and two grooms playing cards by the light of a flickering candle.

They looked up in surprise as he appeared in the doorway and the coachman quickly rose to his feet.

"I wonder if you could help me," Harry asked. "I am His Lordship's guest for dinner tonight and as you can see I am very late. I live around the corner, so it is not worth getting my own carriage out."

He stopped speaking to smile at the men.

"To save me walking round to the front door, I wondered if you would be kind enough to let me in through the garden entrance. I know my way. I have been here before."

"Of course, Sir," the coachman replied. "Oi've got the kay 'ere, 'angin' on a nail."

He led the way across the cobbled yard and opened the door in the high wall which led into the garden.

Harry thanked him, gave him a silver coin, and waited until he heard the key turn in the lock behind him.

Then he ran over the grass towards the house.

He knew the layout and he was aware as he approached it that there was no light in the Drawing-Room or in the Dining-Room downstairs.

He had heard a great deal about Rochfield's manner of entertaining the women he desired.

As he looked up at the lighted windows at the end of the house he had a conviction too strong to be denied that that was where he would find the owner.

There was a solid-looking trellis-work for the roses just coming into bloom which covered the lower part of the house up to the First Floor.

Then, as Harry put his hand on it, he heard Arilla scream.

chapter five

With a strength Arilla was powerless to resist, Lord
Rochfield picked her up in his arms and threw her down on
the bed.

Knocked breathless by the shock of his violence, she
realised that for the moment he was not touching her and
knew she must somehow struggle to get to her feet.

Before she could do so, however, he had flung himself on
top of her.

She realised as he did so that her moment of freedom had
been when he was removing his velvet coat and the scarf
around his neck.

Now, wearing only a thin lawn shirt and long black hose-
pipe trousers, he crushed her beneath him so that she found it
impossible even to scream.

When she attempted to struggle, pushing her hands against
him, she realised, as he tore at her gown, what he intended.

It was then in terror she cried:

"No, no, no!"

But her cry grew weaker and weaker until, with a fear that struck her through like the point of a knife, she realised there was no escape.

"Oh, God . . . help . . . me!" she said in her heart.

At that moment she was aware of a faint noise somewhere in the room, and a second later Lord Rochfield was jerked violently off her body.

In his determination to ravish Arilla, and excited by her resistance, he had no idea that Harry had entered the room through the window.

As he pulled aside the curtains he had seen at one glance what was happening.

Before Lord Rochfield had time to realise Harry was there, he had pulled him violently off the bed and with a hard punch to the chin had knocked him down onto the floor.

For a few seconds Lord Rochfield was unable to find his voice.

Then furiously, lying sprawled on the carpet in an undignified position, he shouted;

"How dare you strike me!"

"If you get to your feet," Harry threatened him, "and fight like a man, I will make sure that you never do this sort of thing again!"

He stood over Lord Rochfield aggressively, his fists clenched, but was too much of a sportsman to hit a man when he was down.

Lord Rochfield's eyes narrowed.

"I will fight you, Vernon, but like a gentleman, and make you apologise for insulting me."

"If that is what you want," Harry replied, "I am only too willing to agree."

"Very well," Lord Rochfield replied, "the usual place in Green Park, at dawn!"

He snarled the words, but at the same time he did not rise, thinking that if he did so, Harry might knock him down again.

"I will be there," Harry said briefly, "and I hope to teach you a lesson which will leave you incapable of behaving in such a dastardly fashion for at least a month or two."

"You are an optimist!" Lord Rochfield sneered, but Harry was not listening.

He had turned to the bed and lifted Arilla, who was struggling to sit up, onto her feet.

He put his arm around her, then, realising that she was so shocked that she was unsteady and almost unable to walk, he picked her up in his arms.

He walked past Lord Rochfield without giving him a second glance into the Sitting-Room, where he set her down.

Holding her closely against him in case she should fall.

"You are all right?" he asked. "It would be a mistake to let the servants know that anything so disgraceful has happened."

"I . . . I am . . . all right," Arilla whispered in a tremulous little voice.

She put up her hands to her hair and as she did so Harry could see that the bodice of her gown was torn.

"Where is your wrap?" he asked.

With an effort she remembered that the footman had taken it from her when she arrived.

"It . . . it is . . . downstairs."

His lips tightened, and leaving her standing for a moment, he picked an arrangement of carnations out of a vase on a nearby table.

He put them into her hands.

She understood and held them against her, even though the stems were wet, as he opened the door.

The candles were flickering in the gold sconces.

With Harry's hand under her elbow, Arilla managed to walk quite steadily and without stumbling to the top of the staircase.

Then as she held on to the banister with one hand, they went down slowly to where the Butler was on duty in the hall as well as the two footmen.

When they reached the bottom of the stairs, Harry said sharply:

"Get me a hackney-carriage!"

A footman opened the door and ran out into the night to obey.

As he went, Harry saw Arilla's velvet wrap lying on a chair and, picking it up, he put it round her shoulders.

He took the flowers from her as he did so, so that she could wrap it over her front, concealing the damage to her gown.

He threw the carnations down on a table and waited impatiently, without speaking, until he heard the wheels of a carriage outside.

Looking at him, Arilla thought she had never before seen a man look so angry, but she was saying a prayer of thankfulness in her heart that he had come in time to save her.

As he assisted her into the carriage he gave the driver the address, then sat down beside her as a footman shut the door.

As they drove off, Arilla said in a voice he could hardly hear:

"Y-you came . . . you saved me . . . I thought I was . . . lost and there was . . . no escape."

"You are all right now," Harry said, "and this will never happen again."

"I . . . I received a message to say that you were . . . delayed and would . . . meet me at Rochfield house."

"I received one to say you had a headache and felt too ill to attend," Harry replied.

Arilla gave a little cry.

"He planned it all! He planned that I should be . . . alone with him, so that he could . . ."

"Forget it!" Harry interrupted. "It is over, and if he tries to do such a thing again, I will kill him!"

"But you are . . . dueling with him!" Arilla cried. "He may . . . kill you!"

"He is a good shot," Harry admitted, "but so am I."

"It must not happen. I will stop it!"

Harry gave a little laugh that had no humour in it.

"That is something you cannot do, nor can anybody else."

"I . . . I thought it was . . . forbidden," Arilla faltered.

"It still takes place, being a convenient way of settling an argument between two gentlemen," Harry explained. "Rochfield is not a gentleman, damn him! But I cannot refuse to meet him."

"Oh, please . . . please . . . think of some way by which you can avoid it," Arilla pleaded. "I cannot bear to think I may be . . . responsible for your being wounded!"

"Do not . . . worry about . . . me."

She gave a little sob, then she asked:

"Where are we . . . going?"

"I am taking you back to Islington," Harry replied. "But I want to have a word with Charles Ledger first. He will be one of my seconds, and I will find another when I have taken you home."

"How can I go home and . . . leave you when you . . . are fighting over . . . me?" Arilla asked.

"It is what you have to do," Harry said lightly, "and I will come and tell you, when it is all over, what happened."

"I will come with . . . you," Arilla said firmly, "even if I have to . . . walk there in my . . . bare feet!"

"You will do nothing of the sort!" Harry insisted. "It is not the thing for women to be present on such occasions."

"Nobody need know that I am there," Arilla protested. "I can wait in the carriage, or else hide in the bushes."

She paused a moment before she went on:

"I swear to you, Harry, that I could . . . not stand . . . the suspense, the . . . horror of not . . . knowing what is happening."

The way she spoke was so intense, and at the same time so pathetic, that Harry thought for a moment.

Then he said:

"Very well, we will see what we can do. Here we are at Charles's house, where he lives with his mother. So you can come in while I get a better conveyance than this."

Arilla did not speak, but clasping her velvet wrap tightly around her, she let Harry help her out of the carriage.

He led her through the porticoed entrance into an impressive marble hall.

"I wish to see Sir Charles alone," she heard Harry say to the Butler.

"I think Her Ladyship's just retired, Sir," the Butler replied, "but I'll tell Sir Charles you are here."

He led the way across the hall into a room which was lined with books and lit by large candles in carved stands which stood on either side of the mantelpiece.

Arilla, however, had no eyes for anything but Harry.

She was looking at him pleadingly, and praying that he would not insist upon her going back to Islington.

She was becoming more and more determined that nothing should prevent her from seeing what happened at the duel.

Neither of them spoke, until a few minutes later Charles came into the room, exclaiming as he did so:

"This is a surprise! I was not expecting you, Harry!"

Then he saw Arilla and added: "Nor you, Lady Lindsey!"

"I have called to ask you to be my second," Harry said quietly.

"Whom are you fighting?"

"Rochfield, and I only hope I cripple him!"

"I suppose he has been up to his tricks again," Charles said. "Where are you meeting him?"

"The usual place, at dawn," Harry answered. "And by the way, Charles, I have had nothing to eat."

"That is something I can certainly provide," Charles said, "and are you hungry, too, Lady Lindsey?"

"No, no, I want nothing!" Arilla replied quickly.

"She had dinner with that devil," Harry explained, "after he had sent me a message to say that the party was cancelled."

He paused a moment, and then continued:

"He also sent another supposedly from my cousin, saying she was unable to dine with His Lordship, as she had a headache."

"So he was doing the dirty as usual! It does not surprise me!" Charles said as he rang the bell.

"This time he has gone too far!" Harry said. "He is lucky I did not murder him on the spot!"

"A lot of people have felt like doing that."

The Butler opened the door.

"You rang, Sir?"

"Yes, Bateson, Mr. Vernon has had nothing to eat. Ask Cook to provide something which can be prepared quickly, and we would also like a bottle of champagne."

"Very good, Sir."

The Butler seemed quite unperturbed at such demands so late in the evening.

As Arilla sank down in a chair as if she felt her legs would no longer support her, Harry said:

"Please, Arilla, let me take you back to Islington."

She did not answer, but merely looked at him, and as their eyes met he said:

"Oh, very well! Charles, you will have to look after her because she insists on being present at this duel, although, of course, nobody else must see her."

"I think that is a mistake."

"I know," Harry agreed, "but in a way it is her duel."

Charles laughed.

"I suppose being your cousin she is as unpredictable as you are. Very well, we will go in the family barouche, and if anything should happen to you, at least we will be there to take you away."

Arilla gave a little cry.

"Oh, please, Sir Charles, do stop this ridiculous, absurd duel! Harry saved me, and I am sure, as he knocked Lord Rochfield down, he will not trouble me again."

Charles's eyes lit up.

"So you knocked him down, Harry! That is something I doubt he has experienced before!"

He laughed before he went on:

"He usually manages to insist on a duel before he is hurt physically, and because he is such a good shot he is invariably the winner which, to say the least of it, is abominably unfair!"

"This time will prove the exception!" Harry said grimly.

"I hope you are right," Charles replied, "but you will need a great deal of luck as well as skill if you are righting Rochfield."

Every word that was spoken made Arilla feel more and more afraid.

Yet she could understand that as a duel was a matter of honour, it was impossible for Harry not to accept Lord Rochfield's challenge.

All she could do was to pray that he would not be hurt.

The two men laughed and talked together while Harry ate an excellent meal provided for him at such short notice.

He insisted that Arilla join them in a glass of champagne.

"I think the best thing," Charles then said, "is for you and me to call on either Anthony or Edward as the other second, and leave Lady Lindsey here."

He paused a moment before continuing:

"My mother is upstairs as a chaperone, and it would be sensible if, while we are away, she lies down and tries to get a little sleep."

"I will do that," Arilla agreed in a low voice, "if you swear to me . . . on everything you hold . . . sacred that you will come back for . . . me and not go to the duel . . . without me."

"I swear," Harry said. "Anyway, I have to go back to my lodgings to change, and since you could not come with me there, you must do as Charles says."

"Whatever happens," Charles said, "no one must know that Lady Lindsey is with us, and I can trust the servants not to talk."

He thought for a moment and added:

"Actually, there is no need for Lady Lindsey to go upstairs. There is a bedroom on this floor which my father used when he found the stairs too much for him."

He led Arilla into a well-furnished comfortable room a little way down the passage.

Once again the two men promised her that they would return for her, and urged her to try to sleep.

She knew that was impossible, but after they had left she took off her shoes to lie on the bed.

Then she started to pray fervently that Harry would not be hurt, and that, although she sensed that Charles was some-what apprehensive, he would win the contest.

She knew very little about duels, although her father had told her that he had fought in one when he was a young man.

He had a very unpleasant wound in his arm for several weeks after it had taken place.

Because she loathed and despised Lord Rochfield, she did not trust him not to try to injure Harry really.

It would be his revenge for the humiliation he had suffered by being knocked down in his own house and prevented from ravishing her.

"He is a wicked and despicable creature!" she told herself.

But that did not make it any less alarming to think of what lay ahead, and what injury he might do to Harry.

Despite their promises, she was growing anxious and agitated as the hours passed.

It was therefore with a feeling of utter relief that she heard their voices in the passage outside.

Harry knocked on the door and came in.

He had changed, she saw, from his evening-clothes into day-clothes.

Although she had heard that some duellists wore black cravats to make them less conspicuous, she was not surprised to see that Harry's was white.

It was, she knew, a flag of defiance.

She got up from the bed and he said:

"There is no hurry! Charles has ordered a carriage and my friend Anthony Burwood will meet us in the Park. Did you sleep?"

"I have been praying," Arilla answered.

She stood looking up at Harry, then said in a very small voice:

"It is . . . all my fault for suggesting . . . that I come to London if . . . anything . . . happens to you . . . I shall want . . . to d-die!"

"Nothing will happen to me," Harry answered reassuringly, "and what you have to pray for, Arilla, is that I make it difficult for Lord Rochfield to pursue you, or anybody else, for a very long time!"

There was a sharp note in his voice as he spoke, which told Arilla that he was still feeling furiously angry over what had happened.

She wanted to cry at his kindness to her and tell him how much it mattered that he cared.

But she knew that it would only embarrass him, and instead she managed with a tremendous effort to say lightly:

"You have always been lucky, Harry, and I am sure all your friends are . . . betting on your . . . good luck at this moment."

"I am not so sure about that!" Harry replied. "Rochfield has a reputation for being invincible!"

"Then make sure that this time he loses!"

Harry laughed and took Arilla back to the Sitting-Room, where they all had another glass of champagne.

"Not too much, Harry!" Charles warned.

"I am not a fool!" Harry answered. "Be sure I intend to have all my wits about me in the face of the enemy!"

He helped Arilla into the big, comfortable carriage waiting for them outside and they drove off.

Both men seemed determined to treat the whole thing as a joke, and they were laughing when they arrived at Green Park.

"Now, you quite understand," Harry said to Arilla, "that whatever happens—and I mean whatever—you must stay here in the carriage and not let anybody see you."

He added very firmly:

"Charles and I are breaking every rule in letting you accompany us, and you must therefore do as I tell you."

"Very well," Arilla said, "but I must be . . . able . . . to see you."

"I will order the carriage to be turned so that you have a view through the trees of everything that happens," Charles promised.

"And Watkins is on the box if you need anything," Harry added.

Arilla knew already that Watkins was Harry's valet.

She thought he was being wise in making sure that he would be well looked after in case he was wounded.

Charles produced a box containing two duelling-pistols, and as the two men climbed out of the carriage, Arilla put out her hand to touch Harry's arm.

"You will take . . . care of . . . yourself?" she asked in a very low voice.

"I am relying on your prayers," he smiled, then followed his friend.

Arilla resisted an impulse to run after them and beg them to take her with them.

Then the carriage moved and she realised the coachman was manoeuvring it a little nearer to the duelling-ground behind the trees.

When finally he had brought the horses to a standstill, she could see through the morning mist that Harry and Charles and another man were talking together.

Coming from another direction were three other men.

She watched them apprehensively and realised that the one in front was Lord Rochfield.

She thought that even in the way he walked there was something very aggressive about him.

She also had the idea that he was positively looking forward to the duel and was completely confident not only of winning, but of wounding Harry as seriously as possible.

"Oh . . . please . . . God . . . help him!" Arilla prayed.

As she did so, the carriage-door opened and Watkins popped his head in.

"Are you all right, M'Lady?" he asked.

"I . . . I am . . . frightened," Arilla admitted truthfully.

"Now don't you worrit yourself about the Master," Watkins said in a soothing voice of a Nanny. "He can always look after 'imself, he can! But I've got everything ready jus' in case he 'as a scratch."

"I do hope he does not."

Watkins looked towards the duelling-ground.

" 'Is Lordship's got 'is reputation to hink of," he said, "but the Master's got Right behind him, an' that's more important than anything."

He grinned at Arilla and shut the door, and she saw him go to stand behind one of the trees.

She knelt by the window and felt the cool air on her face, which was a relief.

She realised, however, that it was still too dark for the duel to start.

The sky was just beginning to lighten.

As it did so she saw another man, who appeared to walk more slowly, come into the centre of the ground.

She assumed that this was the Referee.

She thought, from the slow way he moved, that he was not only older but resenting having to get up so early in the morning.

The sky lightened a little more and the Referee called the two antagonists to him.

Arilla saw him instructing them as to what they had to do, even though they both must know the rules already.

Then as she held her breath, and started to pray frantically, the duel started.

Harry and Lord Rochfield waited back-to-back, their pistols in their hands, for the Referee to give them the order to start walking ten paces before they could turn and fire.

Now very faintly Arilla could hear his voice:

"One . . . two . . . three . . ."

She could only look at Harry and feel her prayers pouring out to him as if they flew on wings.

". . . four . . . five . . . six . . ."

Harry was moving lightly and gracefully.

Although she did not look at Lord Rochfield, she had the feeling that his footsteps would be heavier and in a way more laboured.

". . . seven . . . eight . . . nine . . ."

Now Arilla held her breath and as she did so the Referee said: ". . . ten!" and the two men turned.

The explosions from their pistols seemed to ring out simultaneously.

Yet, she liked to think, although she was not sure, that Harry's was just a fraction ahead.

Her eyes went towards Lord Rochfield and she knew she was right. He had staggered back and she knew Harry had hit him.

Then as she drew in her breath with excitement, she realised that Harry, too, was staggering.

She saw him drop his pistol and put his hand up to his arm.

It was then, forgetting everything except that he was injured, she flung open the door.

She ran through the trees just as she saw Charles help Harry to sit down on the ground.

As she went she realised that somebody was outpacing her, and it was Watkins.

Suddenly she knew as she went on running, from the agony and apprehension she was feeling, that she loved Harry!

Loved him with all her heart as she had done, although she had never admitted it, for a long time.

* * *

"It's all right, M'Lady," Watkins said. "There may be a lot of blood, but it's only a flesh wound."

They were carrying Harry, although he had attempted at first to walk, to the carriage.

Having cut off his coat-sleeve, Watkins had put a pad on the wound, and was now bandaging it.

It seemed to Arilla as if there were blood everywhere.

Seeing Harry look pale and shaken, she felt frightened and helpless in a way she had never felt before.

"What the devil are you doing here?" Harry asked her.

He realised she was standing beside him while Watkins tried to stem the flow of blood from his wound.

"We should have brought a Doctor," Charles said. "It is usual, but Harry said it was quite unnecessary."

"It was very . . . very necessary!" Arilla said. "D-do . . . you think . . ."

She stopped and looked towards the other end of the field, where she could see that Lord Rochfield, who was still lying on the ground, was being attended to by three men.

"You hit him, Harry," Charles said with a note of elation in his voice. "I had better go across and see how bad he is."

"I do not want any 'Sawbones' interfering with me," Harry replied, "I shall be all right. Just get me into the carriage and take me home."

Anthony and Watkins did as he asked, and as they reached the carriage, Arilla said to Watkins:

"We must take him back to the house in Islington so that I can help you nurse him."

"That's a good idea, M'Lady!" Watkins agreed. "In fact, it's somethin' I was a-thinkin' meself."

The morning light coming through the carriage-window showed that Harry had his eyes shut and looked very pale.

As Arilla noticed it, Watkins did, too, and he said:

"You'll find a flask of brandy in me pocket, M'Lady, if you'd be so kind as to take it out."

Arilla realised that his hands were covered in blood, and finding the brandy, she held the flask to Harry's lips.

He took a good pull at it before he said:

"That is better—now, do not fuss—just take me to Half Moon Street."

Arilla looked at Watkins, shook her head, and he nodded to show he understood.

Charles came to the carriage-door.

"There is not enough room for all of us," he said, seeing that Harry occupied most of the back seat, "so Anthony and I will walk, or else cadge a lift from somebody. Are you all right?"

"Quite all right, thank you," Arilla replied.

Charles looked at Harry and said:

"You have done jolly well, Harry! Rochfield has a hole in his arm which will take a month to cure, and he is pretty 'green about the gills'!"

"I am extremely glad to hear it!" Harry managed to say.

Charles turned to Arilla, who was sitting on the small seat.

"Take good care of him," he said, "and let me know if there is anything you need."

"I will, and thank you!" she replied.

He walked away, back to where Lord Rochfield was being lifted off the ground by the three men.

Before the footmen shut the door he asked:

"Where d'you wish to go, M'lady?"

Arilla, in a low voice in case Harry should interfere, gave him the address in Islington.

When they arrived there Harry was feeling too weak to argue as Watkins and Arilla, with the help of the footman, got him out of the carriage.

They more or less carried him up the stairs.

Rose led the way into a comfortable bedroom which Arilla knew was used by Lord Brandon when he came to the house.

After that it was Watkins who saw to everything.

He managed to get Harry undressed, sent for the Doctor who attended the Prince Regent, and had the whole household running about fulfilling his orders.

He insisted that Arilla go to bed, although she wanted to stay up to see if there was anything she could do.

"You'll be no use nursing the Master if you're too tired to keep yer eyes open!" Watkins said. "Now, you go an' 'ave a 'shut-eye' M'Lady, and when you're feelin' rested, I'll leave you in charge while Oi does the same."

He seemed to Arilla more and more like her Nanny. She realised it was impossible to argue with him and what he was saying was good sense.

She therefore undressed and although she had thought it would be impossible, she slept.

* * *

When Arilla awoke, it was luncheontime and she felt guilty at having slept for so long.

"How is Mr. Vernon?" she asked Rose, who came in when she rang the bell.

"Mr. Watkins's very pleased with 'im, M'Lady, and th' Doctor's been and says what he wants is plenty of sleep, so he's given him somethin' to make sure he does!"

"So he is sleeping now?" Arilla asked.

"Like a baby, M'Lady! I've brought your luncheon up-stairs and when you get up you can go to see him."

It said a great deal for Harry's charm, Arilla thought later, that everybody in the house was eager to do what they could for him.

As if it were a matter of course, they waited on him "hand and foot," taking every request from Watkins as a command that had to be obeyed.

She realised, however, when she saw Harry later in the afternoon that although the Doctor's sleeping-potion worked, he had lost a great deal of blood.

He was completely unconscious of everything that was happening.

As she sat at his bedside she felt he was like a child, helpless, and in need of protection.

She also knew that he was very much a man, that she loved him and her whole being went out to him.

Although she tried to tell herself it was madness and something she must repress, she knew that it would be easier to stop the tide from coming in or the moon from shining.

"I love him! I love him!" she told herself. "How can I possibly . . . marry anyone . . . else when I love him . . . so much? Just to look at him makes me . . . thrill as I have never . . . thrilled before in my . . . whole life!"

She deliberately got up and walked to the window, trying to think sanely and sensibly.

She told herself so that there would be no mistake about it that her love for Harry was an impossible dream which she had to forget.

"It was I who thought out this . . . absurd charade, as a means of . . . marrying a . . . rich man and helping him at the same time as . . . myself," she thought. "So if I have to pay for it with an aching heart . . . it will be . . . my own fault!"

There was no consolation, and yet she knew the only way she could help Harry, whom she loved, was to find a rich husband.

Then she could give him the many, many, things he needed.

How could he, who was such a magnificent rider, go on borrowing horses from his friends?

How, when he got older, could he continue to live on charity because otherwise he would starve?

"I must do something for him, I must!" Arilla told herself.

She knew it would mean submitting to the embraces of some other man whom she might detest with the same loathing that she had for Lord Rochfield.

But what was love, unless it meant self-sacrifice? What was love, unless one could help the person one loved, regardless of self?

"I must find someone who will marry me," Arilla told herself.

Then as she walked softly back to the bed all she could see was Harry, with his eyes closed, looking exceedingly handsome.

She knew then that if he kissed her once it would be as marvellous as entering the gates of Heaven.

"I love you! I love you!" she repeated over and over again.

She sat looking at him for the rest of the afternoon.

chapter six

Harry ran a high fever, which was only to be expected. Arilla never left him for two days, while Watkins watched over him at night.

He was very restless, which was because, she thought, his arm was hurting him.

The Watkins said angrily:

"This 'ere stuff the Doctor's given 'im be as good as a sick 'eadache!"

Arilla thought before she said:

"I did not like to interfere, since Sir William attends His Royal Highness, but Mama always thought that honey was a better healer than anything else, and she always used it on me when I had cuts and bruises as a child."

"Well, it couldn't be worse than wot we've got!" Watkins replied.

He fetched some honey from the kitchen and spread it on Harry's wound, which looked red and inflamed.

Not long after that he seemed less restless and the fever went down.

The next morning Watkins, as well as the Doctor, was astonished when they saw the inflammation had practically gone and the wound was beginning to heal naturally.

"That's a real 'slap in the eye' for 'Is Nibs!" Watkins said with relish as Sir William drove away in his smart carriage.

But Arilla was thanking God that Harry was better.

She did not like to admit to herself how upset she had been.

The next day while Harry was sleeping peacefully she was downstairs in the Drawing-Room.

She was writing letters of thanks for the flowers he had received from so many of his friends as well as gifts of fruit.

She thought they at least relieved a call on their money which was dwindling rapidly.

She also had to face the fact that she had not left the house since the duel.

There had, therefore, been no chance of her meeting the potential husband who was to relieve them of all their difficulties.

She, however, set this problem to one side and concentrated entirely on getting Harry better.

She was just finishing a letter to one of his admirers in which she said that he was improving, when the Drawing-Room door opened and Rose announced:

"Th' Countess of Jersey, M'Lady!"

Arilla jumped to her feet, knowing that it was a great honour that the Countess should come herself and not send a groom to enquire.

As she curtsied to her, the Countess said:

"I see you have made yourself very comfortable here,

although it is not really the proper address for a Lady who wishes to be accepted by the *Beau Monde!*"

"I have been accepted, thanks to you!" Arilla replied softly, and the Countess laughed.

"That is true, but as Harry is staying here with you, you must realise that it does not enhance your reputation. The best thing you can do, therefore, is to marry him!"

Arilla looked at the Countess in astonishment, until she realised that of course she was thinking of her as a rich widow as she had been declared to be.

She was just wondering how she could reply, when the Countess went on:

"This would be the perfect solution for Harry in his present position, for he will find nobody else as pretty as you, with a fortune to boot!"

Arilla was still feeling for words as the Countess asked:

"Surely you find Harry attractive? If you do not, you must be the only woman with whom he has ever been concerned who has not fallen head-over-heels in love with him!"

"I . . . I do not think," Arilla managed to say with difficulty, "that . . . I mean . . . anything to Harry . . . except that he is so kind to me . . . because I am . . . his cousin!"

"Nonsense!" the Countess answered. "Like all men, Harry looks after himself."

She stopped to smile at Arilla before continuing:

"I cannot believe he would have taken so much trouble over you if he were not beguiled by your looks and sensible enough to realise that your wealth makes everything easy."

Arilla drew in her breath.

She wanted to say she loved Harry with all her heart, and to marry him would be like being in Heaven.

Then she knew she had to be very careful not to make the

Countess suspicious that she was not what she pretended to be.

With an effort she managed to speak lightly, saying:

"All I have time to think about at the moment is getting Harry back on his feet! He has been running a high temperature for two days, and has lost a great deal of blood."

The Countess sighed.

"Why these young men must injure themselves in this ridiculous manner, I cannot think! But of course anyone as pretty as you, my dear, is bound to be a natural trouble-maker."

"I hope I am not that," Arilla replied.

The Countess looked at her shrewdly.

"I am curious to know exactly what happened. It is unlike Harry to call out anybody as important as Lord Rochfield, and I understand the Prince Regent is extremely annoyed about it."

"Oh, I hope . . . not!" Arilla exclaimed.

"You take my advice," the Countess said, "and marry Harry as soon as he is well enough. Then all can be forgiven and forgotten."

She patted Arilla kindly on the shoulder and left the house, leaving behind a large basket of expensive fruit which was arranged around a pot of caviar.

It was something Harry was now well enough to eat with enjoyment, and as he did so he said:

"I must be going up in the social world if Frances Jersey, of all people, comes to Islington to see me!"

"She seemed to think it wrong that I should be here unchaperoned," Arilla said tentatively, to see what he would reply.

Harry laughed.

"I do not believe the Countess or even that swine Rochfield would consider me much of a danger at the moment!"

"That is true", Arilla agreed, "and you must rest."

"I want to get up," Harry said like a petulant child. "If there is one thing I hate, it is lying about in bed!"

"You cannot get up until Sir William says you may do so," Arilla answered, "and I know Watkins will prevent you from doing too much."

"Watkins behaves uncannily like the Nanny I had as a child!" Harry retorted. "And if it comes to that, so do you!"

"We have been very worried about you," Arilla said quietly.

"It will please you to hear that Lord Rochfield is suffering too," Charles, who called earlier in the day, had reported. "His wound is healing slowly, and hurting him abominably!"

"I wish I had shot his head off!" Harry retorted.

"In which case you would have had to leave for the Continent," Charles replied, "and I cannot believe you would find Paris very amusing, if you could not afford the alluring delights which that City provides, especially for rich men!"

"If I am to keep being told how poor I am," Harry remarked, "I shall find a job as a crossing-sweeper, or perhaps work in the scullery at Carlton House! If nothing else, I would have plenty to eat!"

"You missed a long and elaborate dinner last night with thirty courses," Charles informed him.

"Than Heavens for that, at any rate!" Harry answered.

He spoke so fervently that both Charles and Arilla laughed.

When she was alone, all she could think of was that Harry was really better.

Once he was up she would have to go back to the Balls, Receptions, and Assemblies which were taking place every day.

Now it seemed more degrading than ever that her reason

for accepting the invitations was that she was trying to find herself a rich husband.

"I cannot bear it!" she thought.

But there was no alternative unless she was to go back to the country and starve alone in the Manor.

She was also afraid that Miss Mimi, the owner of the house, might suddenly decide to return home.

In which case Harry would have to go back to his lodgings. Even if she could find other accommodation for herself, she would not be able to see him as much as she could now.

She had asked Rose when she was helping her dress how long she thought her mistress might be away.

"I've no idea, M'Lady," Rose replied. "It all depends on 'Is Lordship. But I did 'ear they might go t' Nice."

"I hear it is a very attractive place by the sea," Arilla remarked.

She was thinking that if Mimi went to Nice, it would be some time before she returned to London.

"I only 'opes Miss Mimi's 'aving a good time," Rose went on as if she were following her thoughts, "and she doesn't 'ear about poor Mr. Harry. She'd be ever so upset!"

Because of the way she spoke, when Harry woke from his afternoon rest Arilla asked:

"Do tell me about the owner of this house. Rose said she would be very upset if she knew you had been wounded."

"Rose talks too much!" Harry said sharply. "Ths house is owned by Lord Barlow, who is a friend of mine."

Because she could not help herself, Arilla said in a low voice:

"If Miss Mimi was rich . . . would you . . . marry her?"

Harry stared at her in astonishment:

"Good Heavens, no! One does not marry the Mimis of this world! But she is a charming and very pretty person, and that is all you need to know about her!"

"But I am curious!" Arilla protested.

"I cannot think why."

"Rose keeps hinting that she is very . . . fond of you . . . or rather . . . in love with you, and I was . . . just wondering . . ."

"Then stop wondering!" Harry ordered. "Ladies of Quality know when to look and when to look away from another woman, and as far as you are concerned, you have never seen or heard of Mimi."

"I . . . I do not . . . understand," Arilla said, bewildered.

Harry shut his eyes.

"I find all this chatter very tiring," he complained.

Because Arilla felt as if he had slapped her, she was silent.

At the same time, she felt even more curious about Miss Mimi than she had before.

She was suspicious that Harry was fonder of her than he wished to admit.

There was an ache in her heart which was not appeased when the Marchioness of Westbury came to call.

She swept into the house looking extremely smart in a hat trimmed with small ostrich feathers and a gown that revealed very clearly her elegant figure.

She was shown into the Drawing-Room, and when Arilla was told of her arrival, she went to greet her rather nervously.

"Good afternoon, My Lady!" she said, dropping the Marchioness a small curtsy.

"I wish to see Harry Vernon," the Marchioness said, "and do not try to prevent me from doing so."

"I have no wish to do that," Arilla replied, "but my cousin is at the moment asleep. As soon as he is awake I will tell him you are here."

She knew the Marchioness debated whether she should insist on Harry being woken up, but instead she sat down in a chair by the fireplace and said:

"I suppose, Lady Lindsey, you realise you have got yourself talked about in a very unpleasant manner? Surely you have more sense than to engender a duel between Harry and Lord Rochfield!"

"It was the . . . last thing I . . . wanted!" Arilla said defensively.

"I wonder if that is true," the Marchioness remarked. "After all, even if you come from the country, you should be intelligent enough not to create an explosive situation between two gentlemen who are both noted as being good shots."

Arilla was sure it was a mistake to discuss what had happened, and tried to change the subject.

"I know you will be glad to hear that Harry is very much better."

"In which case, if you value your reputation," the Marchioness replied, "I suggest you send him back to his apartment. You may be related, but that is not a licence to flaunt the conventions."

"I am sure Harry will do what . . . is right," Arilla replied. "I will go now and see if he is awake."

She left the room as she spoke.

As she went up the stairs she knew that she hated the Marchioness of Westbury, even if she was one of the most beautiful women she had ever seen.

'Of course Harry is in love with her,' she thought. 'It is impossible for him not to be.'

As she reached Harry's room she saw Watkins was there before her and realised he must have rung his bell.

"Did you have a good sleep?" she asked as Watkins patted Harry's pillow with an expert hand, and he sat looking, she had to admit, exceedingly handsome.

The colour was back in his face, and although he was a little thinner, it became him.

"Come and talk to me," Harry said, "and tell me what is n the newspapers. I am too lazy to read them myself."

"You have a visitor."

"Who is it?"

"The Marchioness of Westbury, and she wants to see you."

"I suppose I had better see her," Harry said, "but do not let her stay too long."

Arilla said nothing, but as she went down the stairs again, there was a feeling in her heart that seemed to tear her apart.

She knew it was jealousy.

When she had shown the Marchioness up into Harry's room, she felt she wanted to cry.

"How can I be such a fool?" she asked herself.

She knew the answer to that question was that she loved Harry until it was an agony as well as a joy to be near him.

* * *

The following day Harry insisted he must get up.

"It's too soon, Cap'ain," Watkins protested.

"I am not going to be treated like a child or an imbecile any longer!" Harry retorted. "I will rest after luncheon, as I always do, then I will get dressed and sit in the window."

"Very well," Arilla replied before Watkins could do so, "but if you have a relapse and are forced to spend another week in bed, do not blame us!"

"I am perfectly well," Harry said, "and bored with everybody fussing over me and saying I look like a wounded hero because my arm is in a sling!"

He was teasing, but Arilla knew that one person who would welcome him back was the Marchioness.

She had left the house the previous day looking, she thought, like the cat who had been at the cream.

"What is more," Harry said as Watkins left them alone, "I will not have you sitting at my bedside, playing the part of a ministering angel! What parties have you been asked to tonight?"

"I am not going to tell you," Arilla replied, "because if you are going to get up, we will have dinner together in the *Boudoir*, which means you will not have to climb up and down the stairs."

"How do you know I want to dine alone with you?" Harry asked. "Perhaps I would like a glamorous party with at least a dozen guests."

He paused for a moment, with a smile on his face, before he went on:

"Afterwards we could play cards, or perhaps dance."

Arilla gave a cry of horror until she realised that he was teasing her.

"You can get up for dinner," she said, "but unless I am very much mistaken, you will be glad to go back to bed."

"I will allow you to dine with me," Harry said loftily, "if you promise me that tomorrow you will go back to work. How many invitations have you refused so far?"

"Not so very many," Arilla said, "and quite frankly, I would rather be here with you."

"You know as well as I do," Harry said in what she thought was a hard voice, "that you are wasting time and money, and now on top of everything else, we will have to pay the Doctor's fees."

"Is he very . . . expensive?" Arilla asked in a low voice.

"Very!" Harry replied. "Now, go downstairs and accept all the invitations you hae received for tomorrow when you will be off duty."

Arilla looked at him pleadingly.

"Do not . . . bully me, and you know I shall . . . hate to go to a Ball . . . without you."

"It is something you have to do," Harry said sharply. "At least, from what Charles tells me, you are not likely to run into Rochfield, and it would be a mistake to let your other admirers neglect you."

Arilla did not answer.

She only thought despairingly that Harry was right and the sooner she got back to "work" the better.

She had luncheon on a tray by his bedside.

Then after Watkins had prepared him for sleep, even though he protested at his doing so, she went down to the Drawing-Room to look at the large stack of invitations that had arrived for her.

There was also another pile for Harry which Watkins had collected from his lodgings as well as those that had come directly to the house.

She knew that when she came to London she had been thrilled by the number of distinguished people who had entertained her.

Now the only thing she wanted was to be alone with Harry.

To talk to him, to hear him laugh, and to know that every moment they spent together she fell more and more in love with him.

Finally, because she knew it was sensible and what he wanted, she accepted a number of invitations for the rest of the week, and for the week following.

Then, as she thought she would ask Rose to arrange for someone to deliver her acceptances to the houses concerned, the door opened.

She looked round impatiently, thinking it was a caller to see Harry, who would encroach on the time she could be with him.

Then she heard Rose say in a rather nervous voice:

"Lord Rochfield, M'Lady!"

For a moment Arilla was frozen into immobility, then as

Lord Rochfield came into the room, his arm in a sling, she rose to her feet.

She found it hard to believe he was really there, but as Rose left the room he said:

"I had to see you, lovely lady, and this afternoon is the first time they would permit me to leave my bed."

Arilla thought he looked pale.

But she was so flustered by his unexpected appearance that she could only move towards him, saying as she did so:

"I am sure it is . . . too soon for you to be . . . moving about. Please . . . sit down and . . . perhaps you would like something . . . to . . . drink?"

"A glass of champagne would be very pleasant!" Lord Rochfield answered.

Arilla tugged at the bell-pull.

As the door was opened almost immediately, she guessed that Rose had been waiting outside and very likely listening to what was being said.

Watkins had, of course, related to the household what had happened at the duel.

She could understand that the servants, like herself, were extremely surprised that Lord Rochfield should have called.

She ordered a bottle of champagne, then, feeling nervous, sat down some distance from Lord Rochfield.

"I have been hearing reports on your patient's progress," he said with a slight twist to his lips, "and I understand he is getting better."

"That is true," Arilla said, "and I agree with the Countess of Jersey who thinks it a . . . great mistake that the duel should . . . ever have taken place."

"That comes well from Frances Jersey," Lord Rochfield said sarcastically, "who has had a number of duels fought over her, and although she was an extremely attractive woman, she was not as beautiful as you!"

"All I can say," Arilla replied in a low voice, "is that is something I do not . . . wish to happen . . . again. It has distressed me a . . . great deal."

"I was afraid of that," Lord Rochfield replied.

Because he spoke so pleasantly, she looked at him in surprise.

At that moment Rose came back into the room with the champagne.

Arilla refused a glass, but she handed one to Lord Rochfield and Rose set the tray down on a side-table and withdrew.

"I admit to feeling somewhat unsteady," Lord Rochfield said, "but I could not wait any longer to see you."

Arilla thought that once again he was going to pay her extravagant compliments and stare at her in the way she always considered both impertinent and unpleasant.

She therefore looked away from him, across the room towards the window which opened onto the garden, and said in a low voice:

"I think . . . My Lord, I should be . . . truthful and say that I . . . think it was . . . a mistake that you should . . . come here to . . . see me."

"It is not a mistake as far as I am concerned," Lord Rochfield said, "for I could not wait any longer to ask you if you will do me the honour of becoming my wife!"

For a second Arilla felt she could not have heard him aright.

Then as she turned her head to stare at him in sheer astonishment he said:

"I have managed to avoid matrimony since my first wife died and I swore, because I was exceedingly unhappy in my marriage, that I would never marry again. But I have fallen in love and I find it impossible to think of anything but you."

His lips twisted in a wry smile before he added:

"I hope that if you will forgive me for behaving as I did, we could be very happy together, and I would give you everything in the world you could every want."

It flashed through Arilla's mind that what she wanted was horses for Harry, money for him to be able to live as a gentleman should, and a great many other things besides.

Then as she stared at Lord Rochfield she remembered what she had felt when he touched her.

Once again she could feel the terror he had aroused when he had flung her on the bed, and the heaviness of his body which had held her powerless beneath him.

She had hated him then, and she hated him now, and almost as if he could read her thoughts, he said:

"I never thought I would feel like this, and because I found you utterly desirable, I was determined to make you mine."

He leered at her before continuing:

"It never struck me, because you had been married, that you were so unsophisticated and innocent that you would be appalled by my behaviour."

He paused, and as Arilla did not speak, he went on:

"Thinking it over, and I have had time to do that, I realise I not only have to apologise to you, which is something I have seldom done in my life to anybody.

"I also have to teach you to trust me, and to believe me when I tell you that once we are married I will make you love me."

Listening to him, Arilla felt she must be in a dream.

At the same time, she was clenching her fingers together and forcing herself to listen calmly and not obey her impulse to run away.

"We know very little about each other," Lord Rochfield continued, "but I know that you are everything a man could wish for in his wife and the mother of his children."

His voice deepened as he said:

"Marry me, Arilla, and I swear to you there will be

nothing in the world I will not give you. I will make you happy and there will be no other women in my life!"

He waited for her to reply, but Arilla, drawing in her breath, felt as if her voice had died in her throat.

How could she not be dreaming that Lord Rochfield, who was so rich and important, was, after all that had happened, actually asking her to be his wife?

She wanted to scream in horror at the idea.

Then a pride and a self-control she had not known she possessed came to her rescue.

Looking down at the ground so that he would not see the horror in her eyes, she said:

"I am very honoured . . . My Lord, by what you have . . . said to me . . . but you must . . . understand it is both a . . . surprise and a . . . shock after what . . . occurred."

"I have said I am sorry," Lord Rochfield said harshly.

"I know . . . and I understand it was . . . difficult for you to . . . do so."

Arilla smiled at him before she went on:

"At the same time, it is difficult for me to adjust myself to a situation which I never . . . expected to arise . . . even in my . . . wildest imagination!"

"But it has happened!" he persisted.

"I know . . . but I am sure you will . . . understand that I need time to . . . think, to adjust myself. And just as you were not . . . eager to marry again, I . . . feel the . . . same."

It was a lie, but she managed to make it sound convincing.

As if he realised she was very shy and nervous, Lord Rochfield said:

"I can only ask you, Arilla, to think about what I have said, and to realise it is so important to me that I had to come here today, against my Doctor's orders, simply to tell you what was in my heart."

"I . . . I appreciate . . . that."

"I will give you time," he went on, "but try to believe how happy I shall make you."

He waited a moment, but when she did not speak he continued:

"Do not take too long over your considerations or I think you will drive me mad! I want to marry you at once!"

He paused again before he went on:

"I want to take you away from London so that we can be alone and get to know each other. And once you are mine, I will never let you regret it!"

When he said the word "mine," it brought back to Arilla all the horror she had felt when he had lain on top of her, tearing at her gown.

He had seemed then like a savage animal.

Although she knew he was controlling himself now and doubtless because of his injury he was not as passionate as he had been before, she knew that he had the same fire in his eyes.

She felt herself shrink from him as if he were something degrading and unclean.

"I hate him!" she told herself.

Then once again she was thinking of Harry and how very, very rich Lord Rochfield was.

He finished his glass of champagne and rose to his feet.

"Now I am going to leave you," he said, "and when I call tomorrow I want you to tell me what I am longing to hear."

"I could not . . . give you my answer so . . . quickly," Arilla said.

"When you think over my proposal and when you realise how deeply I love you," Lord Rochfield said, "I know you will understand how much I can give you, and, as my wife, think what your position will be in the Social World."

There was a boastful note in his voice as he went on:

"The Prince Regent looks on me as one of his closest friends, and in the not too distant future, when he becomes

King, he will want me at his right hand. Then we will both enjoy the Hereditary position I will have in the Palace."

It was almost as if he saw it all passing in front of his eyes as he continued:

"You will be proud of me, my beautiful one, and I will be very proud of you. But before this happens I will have time to teach you the joys and desires of love, and it will be very exciting for me."

Now his voice was deep and there was a note in it which made Arilla tremble.

She was sure if she looked at him the fire would be leaping dangerously and she would feel consumed by it.

Like a frightened fawn she rose to her feet feeling she could bear no more.

"I will give you time to think," he said almost as if he spoke to himself, "but I cannot wait too long, Arilla! I want you—I need you!"

Now she was definitely frightened, and, moving nervously towards the door, she said:

"I am sure you should . . . not do too much on your . . . first day out . . . and as your carriage is waiting . . . My Lord, I beg you . . . to go . . . home."

"That is what I intend to do," Lord Rochfield said, "but I shall come back tomorrow, the next day, and the day after that. In fact, every day until you give me the answer I want to hear."

Fearful that he might touch her, Arilla opened the door and he passed through it into the hall, where Rose was waiting.

She watched the maid hand Lord Rochfield his tall hat, his stick, and his gloves.

Then, as she opened the front door, he turned back to where Arilla was standing watching him.

"Good-bye, until tomorrow!" he said. "And remember, I am a very impatient man."

Arilla thought there was a threat in the last words.

As he went through the front door she ran frantically up the stairs and without knocking flung open the door of Harry's bedroom and burst in.

He was out of bed and standing at the window, but he was only partially dressed, and in his shirt-sleeves tying his cravat.

He was alone, and as Arilla came into the room he turned with an expression of surprise.

Neither of them spoke as Arilla stood for a moment staring at him.

Then slamming the door behind her she ran across the room to throw herself against him, hiding her face in his shoulder.

His good arm went round her and he said in a tone of concern:

"What is the matter? What has happened? Why are you upset?"

"Oh, Harry! Harry!"

There was a desperate note in her voice and Harry said again:

"Tell me—what has occurred?"

"L-Lord . . . Rochfield . . ."

Harry's arm tightened.

"What has he done now? Why are you in this state?"

"He . . . he came here!"

"Then he had no right to do so!"

"H-he came . . . to ask me to . . . m-marry him!" Arilla said in a voice that Harry could hardly hear.

For a moment it was as if Harry had been turned to stone.

Then Arilla raised her head to look up at him with tears in her eyes that were dark with fear, and her lips were trembling.

"He . . . wants to . . . marry me! Oh . . . Harry . . . Harry . . . how can I . . . marry him? H-how can . . . I?"

It was the cry of a child frightened in the dark. Harry

looked at her for a long moment before he ejaculated in a voice she could barely recognise:

"Oh, my God!"

Then his lips came down on hers.

Arilla thought she must be dreaming.

Yet, as Harry kissed her passionately, wildly, demandingly, as if he were as upset as she was, she knew that this was what she had wanted but thought impossible.

He kissed her until she felt her whole body respond to him.

He took with his kisses not only her heart, but also her very soul.

She was his, and love seemed to streak through her body like shafts of lightning moving through her breasts and up into her throat, almost painful in their intensity, yet an ecstasy beyond words.

Then they passed from her lips to Harry's and she was no longer herself, but part of him.

Only when she felt that he had given her a rapture that came from Heaven itself did he raise his head and say in a voice she could not recognise:

"How can you do this to me? How can you torture me so unbearably until it is driving me mad?"

"I love you . . . I love you!" Arilla said brokenly. "But I . . . suppose I ought to m-marry him!"

"Damn him!" Harry cursed. "May he burn in hell's fire! How can I lose you now, my darling?"

He pulled her closer still and his other arm, which had been wounded, crept round her and she said:

"Harry . . . be careful . . . your arm!"

"What does it matter what happens to me if I cannot have you?"

He paused to smile at her before he went on:

"My precious, you do not know what I have suffered these last weeks. But how could I have known—how could I have guessed—that Rochfield would want to marry you?"

"H-he has ! . . . everything in the world that I . . . want," Arilla faltered. "Superb horses for you . . . I want you to be comfortable . . . and not have to . . . live on . . . and beg from other people."

Harry gave a laugh that had no humour in it.

"That is what I want too," he siad, "but it is you who would have to marry that swine! And the ghastly truth is, my beautiful, that you will never have an offer from anyone richer or more important."

"I . . . I know that," Arilla whispered, "but . . . nothing matters except that . . . I love you."

"How can you be so foolish, so idiotic as to love someone like me?" Harry asked angrily.

"I love you because you are everything a man should be . . . strong, determined, and, at the same time . . . kind and gentle. Oh . . . Harry . . . how can I . . . ever marry anyone else?"

It was as if they both suddenly felt at the same moment that their legs would no longer support them and they sat down on the bed.

Harry put his arms around Arilla and she hid her face against his shoulder.

"It is all your fault," he said, "for being so ridiculously, absurdly lovely! When you are not with me, I find myself seeing your face everywhere I look, and when you are there, all I can think of is the blue of your eyes."

There was a tenderness in his voice that made Arilla feel as if her heart turned over in her breast. Then she said in a very small voice he could hardly hear:

"If . . . if I marry him . . . it will be only . . . because I . . . love y-you!"

"Dammit, that is not a good enough reason!" Harry said. "There must be other men better than Rochfield!"

"If there . . . are," Arilla said, "it is doubtful if they would be as rich, and I have not yet . . . met them."

She knew without saying any more that both she and Harry were thinking that the little money they had would not last very much longer.

His arm tightened, then as she looked up at him he knew she was wanting his kisses as much as he wanted to kiss her.

He kissed her violently, almost brutally, as if he wanted to hurt her. Yet she felt something wild and wonderful within her respond.

As his kisses grew more and more passionate, Harry moved back onto the pillows, and lifting his feet up onto the bed, pulled Arilla up until she was lying close against him.

Then when their hearts were beating violently and they were both breathless with the intensity of their feelings, he said:

"You are mine—and no other man shall have you!"

"Do you . . . mean that?"

"I mean it!" Harry said. "And I would rather die than give you up!"

"I . . . I feel just the . . . same," Arilla whispered. "I . . . I love you until you fill the whole world . . . the sky . . . and there is nothing and nobody . . . except you!"

"My sweet! My darling! My precious!"

Then he was kissing her again until her body moved against his and she knew the fire in him was also burning within her.

This was love as she had always imagined it to be and as she wanted it, real love, the love that is eternal and a part of God.

Harry released her lips, then he said very quietly:

"How soon will you marry me, my darling, for I know I cannot live without you!"

"And I . . . cannot live . . . without you!" Arilla replied. "But . . ."

"There are no 'buts,'" Harry interrupted, "and if you think I would allow you to marry Rochfield or anybody else,

133

you are mistaken! You are going to marry me, and somehow, although God knows how, we will find a way to live without starving."

Arilla's head fell back against his shoulder as she said in a frightened voice:

"H-how can we . . . do that?"

Harry did not answer, and after a moment she said:

"I thought . . . before you came to . . . rescue me how . . . hopeless it was that I have no way of earning money."

She gave a deep sigh before she went on:

"I am well-educated. Mama saw to that. I can cook if I have the proper ingredients with which to do so. And I can ride very well when I have a good horse under me."

She tried to speak lightly, but there was a little note of despair in her voice.

"I might say the same thing," Harry answered, "except that my only talent is being a good rider."

Suddenly, so suddenly, he gave a cry that made Arilla jump.

"I have it!" he said. "I know what I am going to do, and at least we should be able to eat, even if you have to cook the food, my darling!"

"What . . . what do you . . . mean?"

"I mean that I have, as we both know, a talent for making the most obstreperous horse obey me. In fact, I can break in any horse, however wild it may be!"

Arilla raised her head and stared at him as Harry went on:

"What we are going to do, my precious, is to back our luck in finding horses that can be trained into the best animals that anyone could want to buy!"

Arilla gave a little cry but did not interrupt, and he went on:

"It is not difficult, it needs only patience, and once we can breed from our own mares, there is no reason why we should not make a small fortune out of it!"

Now there was an enthusiasm in the way he spoke which Arilla found infectious.

"It sounds wounderful!" she cried. "And even more . . . wonderful that I can do it with . . . you! But, darling Harry . . . have you forgotten . . . we shall need capital at first . . . capital to buy . . . stallions and mares."

"That is easy!"

"How . . . can it . . . be?"

"We will buy everything we require after we are married!"

Now Harry was smiling and as Arilla stared at him he explained:

"Our wedding presents! They will be the capital with which we will start our business—a business, my darling one, which will be financed and worked by love!"

chapter seven

"Thank You . . . God, thank You . . . thank You . . .!"
Arilla said over and over again in her heart.

After she went to bed, she woke up in the night and
whispered it aloud in the darkness.

At the same time, after the third day of a rapture that made
her feel as if she were floating on the clouds, her conscience
began to prick her.

How could she possibly take Harry away from the world in
which he shone, despite having no money?

When she thought of it, she could see the Manor so
dilapidated with everything in it threadbare or in need of
repair.

The paper on the walls was peeling, the paintwork cracked
and dirty.

"How can Harry," she asked herself, "thrive in a place
like that?"

Then when she thought of his kisses and the feeling they had for each other, nothing else seemed to matter.

"I love you! I love you!" she said to him when she was with him, and his love seemed to envelop her like an aura from which she could never escape.

The second day after he had got up Harry informed her that he was going out.

"It is too soon!" she protested.

"Not for what I have to do."

"And what is . . . that?" Arilla asked nervously.

"The first person we have to tell we are to be married is the Prince Regent," he explained. "He loves being 'in the know' earlier than anybody else."

He stopped speaking a moment, and smiled before he continued:

"He would be furious if he heard rumours that I was about to be your husband before I told him about it."

Harry had helped Arilla compose a clever letter to Lord Rochfield, which he received when he called, as he had promised he would.

Arilla told him that while she was deeply honoured by his offer, she had to think very seriously about marriage, especially after he had frightened and shocked her.

She also said she was deeply perturbed that anybody should know about the duel.

Therefore she felt it only right that she should meet some of her friends, which she had been unable to do recently, before she made such an important decision as to marry again.

It was a kind letter and not in the least aggressive. When she read it over, Arilla thought it would be impossible for Lord Rochfield to be angry or spiteful about it.

She was afraid that, if he was, he might do harm to Harry, and that concerned her more than anything else.

"If he is tiresome, I will challenge him to another duel!"
Harry threatened.

Arilla gave a little cry of fear.

"You will do no such thing! I suffered enough when you were running a high fever, and you may not be lucky every time."

She thought for a moment, then she said in a whisper:

"Suppose he had . . . killed you?"

"He would not do that," Harry replied, "but as I do not want you to be upset, I promise that if we do meet I will try to be polite to him."

"Please . . . promise me . . . that on . . . everything you hold . . . sacred," Arilla insisted.

"I promise on you, which means more to me than anything else!"

Then he kissed her and it was impossible to go on talking about anything except themselves.

When Harry left to see the Prince Regent, his arm still in a sling, he was looking, Arilla thought, because he was happy, even more handsome than ever before.

She went back to the house praying that the Prince would not be angry with Harry, and somehow he could persuade His Royal Highness to give his august blessing to their marriage.

She knew if that happened, although it seemed very mercenary, their presents would be better than they might otherwise be.

As they were to build their whole future on them, it was very important that their friends should be generous.

She moved about the house restlessly, having no wish to see anyone or go out until Harry returned.

When he came back he was hurrying in a way which told her, before he spoke, that everything was all right.

Then as he put his arms around her he said in a voice of triumph:

139

"I have won! I have won, my darling, and you can be proud of me!"

"What have you won?" she questioned in surprise.

"His Royal Highness has not only forgiven me for duelling with Rochfield, but when I told him that you and I are to be married, he said he would give the Reception for us at Carlton House!"

"I . . . I cannot believe it!" Arilla gasped. "And that means . . ."

"It will not cost us a penny!" Harry finished. "And it only needed a little prompting on my part to make him suggest it. Say I am clever!"

"You are brilliant, and I love you!" Arilla answered, putting her arms round his neck.

He kissed her until once again they were floating in the sky. Then Harry said:

"We will announce the date of our wedding the day after tomorrow, and it will take place at the end of next week."

"The end of . . . next . . . week?" Arilla gasped. "How can we be . . . married so . . . soon?"

"'Needs must when the devil drives!'" Harry replied. "The truth is, my lovely one, we have almost run out of money!"

Arilla was still. Then she said:

"Are you certain . . . quite certain you are doing the . . . right thng in marrying me?"

"Are you regretting it already?" Harry countered.

"No . . . no . . . of course not. It is only . . . I cannot bear to think that you will . . . miss all the . . . excitement and gaiety of London . . . and then be . . . sorry that you . . . married me."

She could not prevent giving a little sob on the last words, but Harry laughed and swept her up into his arms.

"Do you think any of that matters beside you?" he asked.

"How could I live in London, seeing you with another man, making polite conversations with you at parties, and going home alone?"

There was a depth in his voice that made what he said sound so sincere that Arilla felt that despite everything, she was doing what was right.

"We were meant to be together," she argued with herself. "Perhaps we met in other lives and have found each other across eternity."

It was what she wanted to believe because she knew that as far as she was concerned, there never was, and never could be any man in the world for her except Harry.

When their engagement was announced in *The Gazette*, nobody seemed to be particularly surprised. They were overwhelmed by the congratulations of their friends.

Arilla knew uncomfortably that they all believed Harry was marrying money and she felt ashamed that they had to deceive people who were so kind.

At the same time, when the presents began to arrive she knew that if they had not been going on display at Carlton House and if the Prince had not given his blessing to their wedding, the gifts would not have been nearly so expensive or so spectacular.

Harry made everyone laugh when at a party the Marchioness of Worthington asked rather spitefully, Arilla thought:

"What is your cousin the Duke giving you?"

"His good wishes, which cost him nothing," Harry replied.

But the majority of his friends made an effort to give him something useful.

When Arilla looked rather wistfully at a fine leather dressing-case with gold fittings, she wished Harry could keep it.

"What am I to do about a wedding-gown?" she asked

Harry. "If we were being married quietly, I would have worn one of the gowns I have already."

She gave a little sigh before she went on:

"But I am afraid women like the Countess of Jersey, who has a very sharp eye, would notice it at once."

"I have fixed that already."

"You have? What have you arranged?"

"Liza is going to give you a gown as a wedding-present."

"I cannot allow her to do that!" Arilla exclaimed, and when Liza came to fit her she said:

"It is too kind . . . too generous of you . . . even to think of such a thing . . . but of course . . . I must pay you . . ."

With difficulty she bit back the words "some time" or "as soon as I can," but before she could say any more, Liza answered:

"It's not only a wedding-present, M'Lady, it's also one of gratitude for what you've done for me."

Arilla raised her eye-brows, and Liza explained:

"Ever since you appeared in the first gown I designed for you, new customers have been flocking to me!"

She paused and gave Arilla a smile before continuing:

"I've sold your green gauze a dozen times and I wouldn't mind betting that every future bride, after they've seen you, will be coming to me for their wedding-gowns."

"I hope so!" Arilla said. "And thank you, very . . . very much!"

"I'm sure I'll be making you lots of gowns in the future, M'Lady," Liza said.

Arilla did not dare to disillusion her.

* * *

The night before their engagement was announced in *The Gazette* she wrote another letter to Lord Rochfield, telling him as kindly as she could that she was to marry Harry.

She wrote:

. . . I have known him since I was a child, but it was not until I came to London that I realised I was in love with him, and that he has always been in my heart.

Please understand and give us your good wishes . . .

There was no written reply from Lord Rochfield.

But he sent them a large and rather ugly silver rose-bowl as a wedding-present which Harry said would fetch quite a considerable amount of money and they should be very grateful for it.

"I suppose really," he said with a smile, "if I had any pride, I would throw it back at him. As it is, the money from it will be a great help, and I shall cherish every penny of it."

By the beginning of the next week there was quite a lot more to cherish.

Every day more and more gifts arrived until Rose said she was worn out with having to answer the door.

At the same time, the whole household was excited at the thought of a wedding, and the food Arilla and Harry ate when they were alone was delicious.

It made her wonder apprehensively if she could ever cook as well when they were at the Manor.

The only person who knew the truth and what they were intending to do was Charles.

"I am going to tell him, darling, because I need his help," Harry explained. "As he will be in London, I can let him know as soon as I have a horse worth selling."

He gave a sigh before he went on:

"I can rely on him to get the highest price possible for it."

"I am only too willing to help you," Charles said when Arilla thanked him, "and to tell you the truth, I always thought it rather strange that you were so innocent and unspoilt, considering you were a married woman."

143

Arilla blushed, and Charles laughed.

"There you are!" he said. "I know of no other woman in the *Beau Monde* who would blush so prettily or look so shy."

"You do not think anyone has guessed that we have been deceiving them?" Arilla asked nervously.

"Not a chance of it!" Charles answered. "They are all convinced that you are rolling in money, and Harry is 'on to a good thing'!"

He saw the expression in Arilla's eyes and said quickly:

"Of course, they know he is also obviously in love with you, and that is very understandable, seeing how beautiful you are!"

Whenever Charles came to the house he and Harry talked incessantly about horses. Where he could buy good yearlings, and who had the best stallions to service his mares.

There were a hundred more details concerning what was necessary to create a market for the horses that Harry would break in.

It was only when she was alone that Arilla felt frightened when she thought of the Manor and the rough ground surrounding it which had never been cultivated.

She was sure Harry was under-estimating the discomfort of living there.

When she tried to tell him of her fears, he said:

"Leave the worrying to me, I am quite prepared to live on love and kisses until I can make enough money to afford a great deal more."

"Suppose . . . darling . . . you do not . . . manage it?" Arilla whispered.

"Are you doubting my capabilities?" Harry asked. "I thought you trusted me!"

"Of course I trust you!" Arilla cried. "I trust you . . . I adore you . . . I think you are . . . wonderful! I am just . . . afraid that you are . . . giving up too much for . . . me."

"What am I giving up?" Harry asked loftily. "Two pokey little rooms in Half Moon Street!"

He stopped a moment, and then continued:

"There are a number of people who are kind and hospitable because I amuse them, and I am eternally at the beck and call of His Royal Highness!"

As if he felt he had been disloyal, he said quickly:

"I genuinely like 'Prinny' and admire him. But he is very demanding, and quite frankly, I want to be my own master, even if the house is dilapidated, the grounds need attention, and my wife is rebellious!"

"That is unfair!" Arilla protested. "I am not . . . rebellious! It is only because I love you . . . so much that I want you to have surroundings that are . . . worthy of you."

"I have a feeling," Harry said, "that that is what I should be saying to you. Instead, I will give you love and kisses and, if that is not enough, you will just have to run away with Lord Rochfield!"

They laughed at this, but Arilla put her arms round Harry's neck and said:

"You know I would never, never leave you! Even if you are bored with me I shall still cling to you and, wherever you go, I shall go. I cannot imagine . . . living without . . . you!

"As I feel the same way," Harry said, "I think we are both on to a good thing!"

Then he kissed her and there was no chance to say any more.

* * *

When their Wedding Day dawned, the sun was shining and Arilla knew it was a good omen.

Harry was no longer living in the house in Islington

because, as he said, people would be shocked now that he was well if they were not under separate roofs.

When she went to bed at night, Arilla would count the days, the hours, and the minutes until she could be with Harry and there would be no more parting.

They were to be married at St. George's, Hanover Square, at noon, and the Prince Regent was to be present, while Charles was to be Harry's Best Man.

The decorations in the Church which were usually paid for by the bridegroom had been taken off their hands by Charles and Anthony.

They both had large estates in the country and had the flowers sent up to London with their gardeners to arrange them.

Arilla's bouquet which was of white orchids and lilies-of-the-valley also came from Charles's home.

While she was thrilled when it arrived because it was so beautiful, she could not help thinking what a good thing it was that it cost Harry nothing.

Her wedding-gown from Liza was so spectacular that she was almost embarrassed to wear it.

But she realised she was a model to display Liza's taste and skill. She knew when she looked at her reflection in the mirror that every woman in the congregation would envy her.

Because she was supposed to be a widow, her gown was not white, but silver, embroidered with *diamanté*, and instead of a veil she wore a little cap on her head to match her gown.

It was a relief not to have a train or bridesmaids, and as she walked up the aisle she realised that every woman was looking at her gown.

She felt sure that Lisa was right in expecting dozens of orders for similar gowns either for a Ball or another wedding.

Almost at the last moment, because there had been so

146

much to think about, Arilla remembered there was nobody to give her away.

"It was stupid of me not to think of it," Harry said when she told him, "and of course I will ask His Royal Highness."

"You cannot do that!" Arilla protested. "Supposing he says 'No'?"

"What does it matter if he does?" Harry replied. "I will just have to think of somebody else."

He stopped speaking to smile at her before he continued:

"We might as well leave with a fanfare of trumpets, and what could be more appropriate than that the Prince Regent should officiate? Actually he loves doing that sort of thing."

To Arilla it was exactly like a fairy story that she should be taken up the aisle by the heir to the throne.

She was sure that there would be a lot of envious and spiteful remarks made about her in consequence, but she would not be there to hear them.

Once she and Harry had left London, no one except Charles was to know where they had gone or what they were going to do.

"I have hinted," he said to Harry, "that you are going abroad. Quite a number of people think Paris is just the right place for a honeymoon."

"That was a good idea," Harry said, "but you must be very careful, Charles, not to let anyone have the slightest idea where we actually are."

He paused and chuckled, before he went on:

"Otherwise they might take it into their heads to visit us, and once they saw the Manor they would certainly know that Arilla has no fortune!"

"You can trust me," Charles said, who'd been told the truth a few days ago, and was touched by their circumstances rather than shocked. "Actually I think you are both magnificent! It takes a great deal of courage to do what you are doing, which is something I do not believe I could do myself."

"You would—if you were to be married to Arilla!" Harry said smilingly.

There was such an expression of love in his eyes that Arilla felt the tears come into her own.

* * *

As the Bishop of London married them, Arilla prayed fervently to God and to her father and mother for help so that she could make Harry happy.

"No other man would do what he is doing," she said in her heart, "and I can only be certain that he has no regrets if I am helped by the Divine Power which I feel when he kisses me."

She and Harry looked very radiant when they came down the aisle together.

Even the most sophisticated women in the fashionable congregation felt a little constriction in their throats and a sudden moisture in their eyes.

Charles said afterwards that he had never known a Reception where there was so much laughter.

Everybody seemed infected by the happiness which vibrated from the bride and bridegroom.

The Prince Regent made a witty speech which he himself enjoyed as much as everybody else did, and Harry replied.

He, too, was witty, but at the same time managed to thank everybody who had been so kind to them with a sincerity which warmed their hearts.

Only Arilla and Charles knew he was thinking of the magnificent display of presents which were laid out in the Chinese Room.

The money they would get on disposing of them would have to keep them for a very long time.

Only when they drove away in the carriage which once again had been borrowed from the absent Lord Barlow did Arilla say:

"Where are we going? I meant to ask you, then forgot."

"We are going to have one more night of luxury in Islington," Harry answered. "I have sworn the servants to secrecy, nobody will come near us, and I shall have you to myself."

He smiled as he went on:

"We will be eating delicious food, sleeping in a really comfortable bed, and not until tomorrow shall we face all the difficulties and problems which lie ahead."

"Are you very . . . very apprehensive about . . . them?" Arilla enquired.

"Why should I be, when I have you?" Harry answered.

He did not kiss her as she expected, but instead kissed her fingers one by one, then the palm of her hand.

The only thing they had had to buy for their wedding, Arilla thought, was the wedding-ring.

She had been wearing her mother's ring, but Harry insisted that he intended to chain her to him by every Act of Parliament, and cast a lucky charm so that she could never escape.

"As if I would . . . want to!" she protested.

"I am afraid, because you are so lovely, so perfect in every way," he said, "that there will be a million men like Rochfield, who will try to take you away from me!"

He kissed her then in a possessive, demanding manner which told her it was a real fear.

She wanted him to go on treasuring her, protecting her, and keeping her captive for ever.

They drove back to Islington.

When they had thanked the coachman and the footman, they made them promise they would not say a word to anybody about where they had taken them.

Then as they entered the house Rose bolted and barred the door behind them.

They went into the Drawing-Room which was decorated very touchingly with flowers that had been bought by Rose and the other members of the household.

Harry took Arilla in his arms, saying as he did so:

"Now I want to look at my bride. Is it really true, my beautiful one, that you are mine?"

"That is what I keep on . . . asking . . . myself," Arilla whispered.

"I love you!" Harry said. "I am sure if people knew the truth of what we are doing they would think us both crazy and extremely reckless, but I am not afraid of the future, and I do not want you to be."

"I am only so ecstatically . . . happy that I am . . . your wife, that I can think of . . . nothing else."

"Nor can I," Harry answered, "and that is why I am not going to wait any longer, my darling one, to show you how much I love you!"

They went upstairs hand-in-hand and Harry helped Arilla to take off her wedding-gown.

Then, knowing there were three hours before they would dine, he lifted her into the bed.

"I have dreamt of this!" he said as he kissed her.

She moved as close to him as she could, and he went on:

"I will be very gentle, my innocent little bride, as I have no wish to hurt or shock you."

"You could . . . never do . . . that," Arilla said. "I love you, and when you touch me, I feel shafts of sunshine running through my body."

She paused and gave a little sigh before she went on:

"I want you to kiss me . . . and go on . . . kissing me for ever . . . and ever."

Harry gave a strangled laugh.

Then he was kissing her as she wanted and suddenly the divine light of the sun seemed to envelop them both.

It was to Arilla as if she could hear the angels singing as she had thought she heard them in the Church, and the whole world was lost.

There was only Harry, his arms, his lips, and their love which as they became one, carried them into the very heart of the sun.

* * *

As Arilla awoke and realised that Harry was beside her, she felt her heart leap with happiness.

Last night had not been a dream, it was true!

She was Harry's wife, and it was the most wonderful, perfect feeling she had ever imagined.

He was fast asleep and as she moved very cautiously closer to him she thought of the rapture she had experienced when he made her his.

For the first time she had understood what Lord Rochfield had intended, and knew that if he had ravished her, she would have wanted to die.

With Harry she wanted to live, and have him make love to her for the rest of their lives.

They had dined last night in the *Boudoir* and she found it also decorated with flowers.

Harry had arranged that Rose should bring them dinner, then leave them alone so he could wait on Arilla, and kiss her between every course.

It was difficult to remember what she had eaten.

She thought it was ambrosia and the wine they drank was nectar, and that they were not in Islington, but on Olympus and were one with the gods.

When dinner was over and Harry had taken her back to bed

they found the whole world had disappeared completely, leaving them in the light that came not only from God but also from themselves.

She had never imagined that she was capable of such exquisite sensations, or that love could be so wonderful that it was impossible to express the glory and ecstasy of it.

She did not know whether she said the words "I love you!" over and over again, if Harry had said them, or if the words just seemed to be murmured in the air around them.

She knew only that nothing could be more beautiful, more perfect, more divine than being Harry's wife.

* * *

Harry stirred, then as if he suddenly became aware that Arilla was beside him, he drew her closer.

"Are you happy, my darling?" he asked.

"I am so happy that I feel I must have died . . . died and am . . . now in . . . Paradise!" Arilla whispered.

"That is where we were last night," Harry said, "and I know, my lovely wife, it is something we will never forget."

He kissed her very gently, then he said:

"I told Rose that when I rang the bell she was to bring us some breakfast, which we will have in the *Boudoir*. Then we must leave for the country."

He paused to kiss Arilla's eyes, then the tip of her nose before he said:

"But first, I want to tell you this morning of all mornings, that I am the happiest man in the world, and the luckiest to have married you!"

Then before Arilla could speak, his lips were on hers.

They were clinging together, and once again the room was filled with sunshine, and it was also burning inside them.

* * *

152

Later they went into the *Boudoir* and Rose brought in their breakfast.

It was quite a substantial one, Arilla noticed.

She feared that Harry might be thinking that the luncheon they would take with them as a picnic would be the last rich and luxurious food they would eat for a long time.

Then she knew it was a great mistake to make comparisons.

As Harry had said, she must look on the future as an adventure and a challenge.

She prayed that they would eventually triumph over poverty.

Because she was so happy it would be easy to thrust away any thoughts but the fact that she and Harry were together. He was looking more handsome than he had ever looked before.

He was wearing a long robe which was frogged, so that it gave him a dashing, almost Military appearance. Arilla wished she had seen him in his uniform.

"If you are thinking of me," Harry remarked, "I am thinking of how beautiful you look this morning, my darling!"

He paused a moment to drink in her beauty before he carried on:

"I admire you with your hair falling down your back and wearing what I consider to be a very alluring and seductive *Négligée!*"

"It was another gift from Liza," Arilla explained, "and I feel rather guilty that the only other person who will see it will be you, so she is not likely to get a great number of orders from it!"

"I consider it is more important to please me than anybody else!" Harry said.

"Do you really want me to put that into words?" Arilla asked provocatively.

He reached out his hand towards her but as he did so the door opened and Watkins came into the room.

"What is it?" Harry asked.

"I'm sorry to disturb you, Cap'ain," Watkins said, "but there's a man downstairs as insists on seein' you!"

There was silence. Then Harry asked:

"What does he want?"

"'E wouldn't say, Sir, jus' that it's extremely urgent he should see you immediate-like!"

Harry was still, and Arilla looked at him nervously.

She knew that he was worried, and she could not bear to think that anything should spoil their happiness today.

"If he wants to see me, he had better come and see me!" Harry said grimly. "Bring him up, but he must be quick about it! We are leaving immediately we are dressed for the country."

"O'll fetch 'im, Sir."

As Watkins left the room Arilla asked:

"What do you think this man wants? I thought . . . nobody knew we were . . . here!"

"So did I," Harry agreed, "but I have the uncomfortable feeling that one of my debts has caught up with me."

"You mean . . . he is a Dun?"

"I am afraid so," Harry answered. "I certainly cannot pay him now, and I only hope to God it is not a large sum!"

Arilla thought despairingly that if the money from the wedding-presents had to be whittled away, there would be not much left for the yearlings and mares which Harry had planned to purchase.

Once again she was praying that it would not be anything very serious.

They sat in silence until the door opened and Watkins appeared again to show the man in.

He was middle-aged with hair that was going grey. Arilla

154

thought he looked like somebody who might be concerned with the Law.

She felt as if a cold hand squeezed her heart.

"Good-morning!" Harry said. "I understand you wanted to see me urgently."

"That is right, Sir," the man replied, coming farther into the room.

There was a pause before he came nearer still to Harry before he said:

"I am afraid, Mr. Vernon, I am the bearer of bad news."

"Bad news?" Harry questioned, obviously on the defensive.

"It is with deepest regret that I have to inform you that your cousin the Duke of Vernonwick was killed yesterday morning."

"Killed!" Harry ejaculated. "What happened?"

"The roof of the West Wing collapsed as His Grace was inspecting it, and the Marquess of Vernon was with him when the rafters fell, killing them both."

Harry sat stunned into silence, and their visitor continued:

"My name is Matthews, and I represent His Grace's Solicitors—Matthews, Fisher, and Colby. You will understand Sir, that you are now the Fourth Duke."

He smiled at Harry before he continued:

"We would be greatly obliged if you could see your way to coming as soon as possible to Vernon Park to arrange for the Funeral to take place, and to take over possession of the house and estate."

Arilla saw Harry draw in a deep breath, and as if he understood, Mr. Matthews went on:

"Things are rather difficult, Sir, because of His Grace's ceaseless pre-occupation with economy."

"I presume that is why the roof fell on him!" Harry managed to say at last.

"Exactly, Sir. The house and the grounds also are in a very poor state of repair, while many of the pensioners are unpaid and, through no fault of their own, suffering penury and terrible privations."

He took a deep breath and went on:

"I know there are very large sums of money in the Bank which His Grace refused to invest."

Slowly Harry rose to his feet.

"I understand exactly what you are saying to me, Mr Matthews," he said, "and I assure you it is something which with your assistance, shall be put right as quickly as possible."

A smile transformed Mr. Matthews's grim face.

"That is good news! Very good news indeed!"

He paused a moment and then continued:

"It has been very difficult for us to administer His Grace's affairs when he would not allow us to spend any money or take any advice we offered him."

It seemed to Arilla, watching Harry, as if he suddenly grew in stature.

There was a new authority about him she had never seen before.

"What I want you to do for me, Mr. Matthews," Harry said, "is to procure from Jackson's Livery Stables the fastest Phaeton and the best team of four horses available. Also a brake to follow with my Valet."

He paused before continuing:

"It will take my wife and me about four hours to drive to Vernon Park, but we shall be there as early as possible this afternoon." He looked at Arilla and went on:

"If you and your partners will meet me at the house, we will do our best to 'set the wheels in motion' and rectify as soon as possible the state of affairs you have described."

Mr. Matthews bowed.

"I will do exactly as you say, Your Grace, and thank you.
Thank you very much for relieving us of what has been a
heavy burden of anxiety these past years."

He went to the door, bowed again, and asked:

"At what time would Your Grace like the Phaeton to be
here?"

"In about two hours," Harry replied.

"I will do my very best, Your Grace."

As he was about to pass through the door, Harry asked:

"How did you find me?"

"Immediately I arrived in London late last night I went to
Carlton House," Mr. Matthews replied. "The Steward of the
Household informed me that as Your Grace's bride has been
living here, he was sure the servants would know where her
luggage was going."

Harry laughed.

"As easy as that!"

"Yes, Your Grace."

The door shut and Harry turned to look at Arilla.

"It . . . cannot be . . . true!" she murmured.

"That is what I am telling myself," Harry said, "but it is
all due to you, my darling."

He gave her a long look before he carried on:

"You have brought me luck, the luck I never expected and
never imagined would ever be mine."

"I . . . I hope that is . . . true," Arilla said. "But now that
you are so important and so rich . . . will you . . . really want
. . . me?"

Harry laughed, and it was a very happy sound.

"Are you really asking me such an absurd question? Of
course I want you! We shall be working together very hard,
but in a different way from what I had planned."

He put his hand to his forehead as if it helped him think as
he went on:

157

"There will be a thousand problems to solve, and since
know that the house and the estate are even more dilapidate
than the Manor, it is going to take time. But at least now w
can afford it."

He drew in his breath and went on:

"You heard Mr. Matthews say there are large sums o
money in the Bank uninvested. I always knew my cousin wa
rich and that is why I could not understand why he should b
so cheese-paring and miserly."

Harry spoke as if he were talking more to himself than t
Arilla.

Then as he walked to her side he pulled her to her feet an
into his arms.

"Are you wondering why I told Mr. Matthews to have th
Phaeton here in two hours time?" he asked softly.

"I . . . I thought it was . . . strange, as it will not take . .
us so long to . . . dress."

"We are not going to dress—not yet! This is the mornin
after my wedding. Funerals, estates, and money must all wai
for love!"

He lifted her up in his arms as he said:

"The love and kisses you promised me, darling, an
nothing and nobody is going to prevent me from enjoying
them."

Then as Arilla gave a little cry of excitement because sh
knew what he intended, he carried her back to bed and lai
her down carefully against the pillows.

As he joined her and drew her into his arms the sunshin
once again enveloped them and she knew Harry was right.

Nothing was more important at this moment than themselves and the love and kisses which would carry them into
Paradise of happiness.

"I love you . . . oh, Harry, I love you," she whispered.

"You are mine," he said fiercely, "mine now and forever. Give me yourself."

"I am . . . yours . . . all yours!"

Then they were flying into the heart of the sun, and as the golden glory of it enveloped them, there was only Love and more LOVE for all Eternity.

ABOUT THE AUTHOR

Barbara Cartland, the world's most famous romantic novelist, who is also an historian, playwright, lecturer, political speaker and television personality, has now written over 450 books and sold over 450 million books the world over.

She has also had many historical works published and has written four autobiographies as well as the biographies of her mother and that of her brother, Ronald Cartland, who was the first Member of Parliament to be killed in the last war. This book has a preface by Sir Winston Churchill and has just been republished with an introduction by Sir Arthur Bryant.

Love at the Helm, a novel written with the help and inspiration of the late Admiral of the Fleet, the Earl

Mountbatten of Burma, is being sold for the Mountbatten Memorial Trust.

Miss Cartland in 1978 sang an Album of Love Songs with the Royal Philharmonic Orchestra.

In 1976 by writing twenty-one books, she broke the world record and has continued for the following nine years with twenty-four, twenty, twenty-three, twenty-four, twenty-four, twenty-five, twenty-three, twenty-six, and twenty-two. She is in the *Guinness Book of Records* as the best-selling author in the world.

She is unique in that she was one and two in the Dalton List of Best Sellers, and one week had four books in the top twenty.

In private life Barbara Cartland, who is a Dame of the Order of St. John of Jerusalem, Chairman of the St. John Council in Hertfordshire and Deputy President of the St. John Ambulance Brigade, has also fought for better conditions and salaries for Midwives and Nurses.

Barbara Cartland is deeply interested in Vitamin Therapy and is President of the British National Association for Health. Her book *The Magic of Honey* has sold throughout the world and is translated into many languages. Her designs "Decorating with Love" are being sold all over the U.S., and the National Home Fashions League named her in 1981, "Woman of Achievement."

In 1984 she received at Kennedy Airport America's Bishop Wright Air Industry Award for her contribution to the development of aviation; in 1931 she and two R.A.F. Officers thought of, and carried, the first aeroplane-towed glider air-mail.

Barbara Cartland's Romances (a book of cartoons) has been published in Great Britain and the U.S.A., as well as a cookery book, *The Romance of Food*, and *Getting Older, Growing Younger*. She has recently written a children's pop-up picture book, entitled *Princess to the Rescue*.

BARBARA CARTLAND

Called after her own
beloved Camfield Place,
each Camfield Novel of Love
by Barbara Cartland
is a thrilling, never-before published
love story by the greatest romance
writer of all time.

November '87...THE LOVE PUZZLE
December '87...LOVE AND KISSES
January '88...SAPPHIRES IN SIAM
February '88...A CARETAKER OF LOVE
March '88...SECRETS OF THE HEART

More romance from

BARBARA CARTLAND